EX LIBRIS

VINTAGE **CLASSICS**

TICKY

Stella Gibbons was born in London in 1902. She went to the North London Collegiate School and studied journalism at University College, London. She then spent ten years working for various newspapers, including the *Evening Standard*. Stella Gibbons is the author of twenty-five novels, three volumes of short stories and four volumes of poetry. Her first publication was a book of poems, *The Mountain Beast* (1930), and her first novel *Cold Comfort Farm* (1932) won the Femina Vie Heureuse Prize in 1933. Amongst her works are *Christmas at Cold Comfort Farm* (1940), *Westwood* (1946), *Conference at Cold Comfort Farm* (1959) and *Starlight* (1967). She was elected a Fellow of the Royal Society of Literature in 1950. In 1933 she married the actor and singer Allan Webb. They had one daughter. Stella Gibbons died in 1989.

STELLA GIBBONS

Ticky

VINTAGE BOOKS
London

Published by Vintage 2021

2 4 6 8 10 9 7 5 3 1

First published in Great Britain by Longmans, Green & Co. Ltd in 1943

Vintage
Random House, 20 Vauxhall Bridge Road,
London SW1V 2SA

www.vintage-classics.info

Addresses for companies within The Random House Group
Limited can be found at: www.randomhouse.co.uk/offices.htm

The Random House Group Limited Reg. No. 954009

A CIP catalogue record for this book
is available from the British Library

ISBN 9780099529354

Printed and bound in Great Britain by Clays Ltd, Elcograf S.p.A.

The authorised representative in the EEA is Penguin Random House Ireland,
Morrison Chambers, 32 Nassau Street, Dublin D02 YH68

Penguin Random House is committed to a sustainable future for
our business, our readers and our planet. This book is made from
Forest Stewardship Council® certified paper.

To 198380 and the rest of the British Army

'There is, perhaps, no species of society so striking and
so captivating to the young man entering on life
as that of a military mess'
Ours, Charles Lever

'There aren't better stuff to make soldiers out of
nowhere than Englishmen, God bless 'em! but they're
badgered, they're horribly badgered'
Under Two Flags, Ouida

CHAPTER I

BY the middle of the nineteenth century there had been no soldier in the family of Molloy of Arnewater, a poor estate in the west of Ireland, for twenty years. He therefore decided that his eldest son, Barry, should become one; and with his last thousand guineas purchased for the young man a commission in that most famous of English regiments, the First Bloods.

Barry was pleased at his prospects, for he had been afraid of growing into a squire like his father, who hunted and drank and grew old, but did nothing more. He was so ambitious that his ambition was dear to him as a secret love would have been to a young man with a softer nature, and he never spoke of it. He wanted very large sums of money, the friendship of titled and distinguished men, the love of beautiful women who were also famous. He was twenty, and his dreams were titanic.

But the purchase of the commission had used up, for the time being, his father's resources. Barry would have only his pay to live on. He could not even take with him to London a new Bloods uniform of violet cloth adorned with copper lace; he must wait until he reached London, where, he supposed, any tailor would give credit to a lieutenant in the First Bloods.

However, his father could mount him well, and did: he took with him a stallion named Bayard, whose bright chestnut coat matched Barry's own curling hair.

Unfortunately, the luxurious accommodation that the young man insisted upon for himself and his mount during their journey to London swallowed up the three guineas which was the parting present from his mother, and when he at last arrived in the metropolis, after a long and exhausting journey, he was penniless.

It was a louring and sultry afternoon in late summer.

7

The immense cavern of the railway station was almost in twilight and also clouded with steam. Barry stood still, with his hand on the neck of the horse, while old women with baskets, bearded clerks in top hats, and stout prosperous merchants from Dulwich and Camden Town moved out of the station. Once or twice he checked the stallion's impatient movements with a murmur.

At last everyone had gone, and he was alone. His height and pallor and unusual personal beauty (which was adorned rather than obscured by a travelling cape and deerstalker cap of intimidating cut) made him a most striking figure; and three times porters slouched up to him demanding that they should take his baggage or call him a cab. But he haughtily declined by a slight inclination of his head.

He was trying to think out a plan by which he could arrive at the Bloods' headquarters in a dignified and appropriate manner. He would not make his first appearance on foot and leading a restive horse, nor could he ride in a travelling cape and deerstalker cap. And how should his trunks be conveyed?

He could not hit on a plan. He was so hungry that he felt faint and could not think clearly. He stood still, noticing vaguely that the light in the station had grown dimmer and a hush had crept over the scene, while the noise of hoofs and the rolling of wheels outside the building sounded louder in the stillness.

Suddenly he observed someone in a top hat peering at him over the top of a blind, while a porter was eagerly talking to the top hat and pointing at him. The top hat was the stationmaster. In a moment Barry would be the centre of a scene.

The top hat disappeared from the window and at once reappeared at the office door. The stationmaster, trying not to look as if he were doing so, began to advance upon Barry.

I shall refuse to speak, decided the young man wildly (like many ambitious persons he lacked humour). It's the only dignified thing to do. A terrible pang of disappointment possessed him for a moment; how splendid had been his vision of his entry into the capital! For a year he had been dreaming of it, and here he stood, hungry, angry and penniless, because he had been too proud to sleep in the second-best bedroom at The Two New Potatoes in Dublin and to travel second-class on the train.

The station was now empty, save for Barry, the horse, the advancing stationmaster and the porters, leaning on their barrows like vultures on their nests and gloatingly awaiting the gorgeous row that was blowing up. It was not every day that they saw a swell in a fix.

A low roll of thunder sounded far away.

The stationmaster was now near enough for Barry to see that his whiskers were not black; rather were they a rich brown. He advanced steadily, a lonely figure in a blue frock-coat whose buttons gleamed in the louring stormlight. A second peal of thunder, louder and nearer, rolled round the sky.

Suddenly, at the far end of the station, the figure of an unusually tall man appeared, walking so quickly that his golden beard blew back from the breast of his violet and bronze uniform as he moved.

He careened down the platform, and reached his goal a full yard ahead of the stationmaster. As he put up a glass to a large sleepy blue eye, a third roll of thunder sounded overhead.

"Aw, how de do?" said the giant, saluting. "Lieutenant Molloy, I imagine? Should have been here to meet you but the stweets are cwowded. Her Majesty's dwiving in the Park and all the moleskins are out. Faugh! This your beast, I imagine?"

Barry had returned his salute with one as correct, feeling the cramp and chill slowly recede from his heart as he did so. He had made a fool of himself for nothing. I must learn to control myself properly, he thought fiercely. No one knew that he had made a fool of himself, but that did not console him.

"My name," added the officer easily, "is Venner. Captain Gabwiel Venner, at your service. Nice beast, good boy," he added to the horse. He took no notice of the stationmaster, who had removed his hat, knelt down, and was making a speech, surrounded by the porters who were also on their knees. Barry took no notice either. The beautiful horse and the two tall men stood in calm silence while the thunder crashed; and a horse-box, pushed by a thin little man in the dress of a waiter, came slowly down the platform. It was followed by two more, each pushed by a thin little waiter.

"We'll wide," said Gabriel, and slightly moved one finger, without turning his head, in the direction of the little men, who at once sprang to open the horse-boxes. Out pranced two superb black geldings.

"Your beast must be tired. You'd better wide, had you not, dear old boy?" said Captain Gabriel, caressing the chestnut's nose. "What's his name, Molloy?"

"Bayard," said Barry, smiling and coughing slightly.

"Charmin'."

"I should appreciate it if he could ride. I think the journey has tired him," said Barry.

"Of course he must wide."

One of the little waiters, staring at the gutter, said in a low voice:

"All ve way to ve Club, Capting?"

"Natuwally," replied Captain Gabriel, in a cold tone and without looking at him.

"But it's raining, Capting."

"Natuwally. A storm is in pwogwess. Pway mount, Molloy. If we wide fast we may just be in time to see Her Majesty dwive past the Club."

Her Majesty! The Club! What visions were about to take to themselves a body! Barry's heart beat faster as he put one foot on the quickly outstretched neck of one of the little men and sprang to the saddle. He did not quite like to ride the black gelding in his cape and deerstalker, but of course Captain Gabriel knew what could safely be done without injuring the prestige of the Regiment.

The latter now put his foot on a little waiter's neck in his turn, and lightly mounted. The two gentlemen rode off; and the three little waiters took out three shabby tall hats, which they had held concealed behind their backs while in the presence of Captain Gabriel, and put them on. They then began to coax Bayard into the horse-box, and after this was done they set off slowly in pursuit of the officers.

The summer rain did not blur the beauty of the city, whose trees were fully out and swinging their branches heavy with wet leaves. The houses were brown or grey or of the cream of honeysuckle petals. Down the wide streets raced spanking victorias, drags, cabriolets, fiacres, their red or yellow wheels spinning and sparkling in the glittering rain. In the west there were beginning the pure colours of a rainbow. Gabriel and Barry sat easily in their saddles with the rain dashing in their faces. No rider ever forgets a ride in warm summer rain. They glanced at one another and smiled.

"Capital, ain't it," said Gabriel.

They turned their horses in through the gates of the Park. The blossoming shrubs were out, and every tree sheltered groups of people: and against the rails on either side of the Row was pressed a mob of men and women, dressed in rags and wearing caps made of mole fur.

CHAPTER II

A MOMENT later Barry could look at nothing except the Club.

The mighty building with its twin glass towers glittered darkly against the heavens, which were still partly obscured by flying clouds. The North Tower, indeed, was temporarily concealed in mists from which its pointed summit emerged, remote and awesome as a mountain peak.

Barry stared, endeavouring to subdue the feelings of reverence, gratitude and awe which filled his spirit, for such emotions are of little or no use in a well-planned career.

As they approached the wide gravelled court in front of the Club, which was surrounded by iron railings, Captain Gabriel observed:

"The moleskins are getting a bath to-day, willy-nilly." He set his horse at the crowd and spoke over his shoulder, "They are even more disagweeable when they are wet than when they are dwy. Come!"

The crowd parted to let them through, though unwillingly and with many a sullen oath, and they had just reached the gates leading into the courtyard when a man cried, "Huzza! The Queen, God bless her!" and flung his moleskin cap into the air.

Instantly the air about Gabriel and Barry was full of unsavoury caps which their owners threw up with a dexterous twist that ensured a safe return, and they both turned their horses to see who was coming.

The rain had almost ceased, but the thunder still rolled overhead and a superb rainbow spanned the sky to the west, losing its curve in a grove of mighty elm trees whose branches still sighed in the wind of the dying storm.

"The Queen! The Queen!"

A low open carriage ran smartly between the lane of cheering people, driven by an upright little figure in a magenta dress. Barry caught the gleam of a shrewd grey eye; a plump hand raised a whip perhaps three inches in greeting to Gabriel, who sat immovably at the salute. The lady opposite the Queen was doing nothing, not even looking at the crowd; she was a slender form in a white crinoline, whose face was shaded by a bonnet covered in white ostrich plumes.

"The Queen . . ." muttered Barry, staring after the carriage as it rapidly dwindled away in the direction of the fading rainbow. "Who was the lady with her, pray?"

"Miss Beatwice," answered Gabriel, colouring deeply. "Miss Beatwice Pwessure. She is a lady-in-waiting to Her Majesty."

Barry said no more. He had observed the blush and wished to show that he could be tactful. As they cantered across the forecourt and through the open door of the Club into a dim hall whose roof was lost in shadow, Gabriel continued:

"Miss Beatwice is the daughter of Doctor Pwessure. He is headmaster of the Militawy School in the gwounds here," and Gabriel sighed.

Barry asked no more questions. Gabriel now drew his pistol and fired at a large bronze gong hanging against the wall.

At once echoes sprang up in every corner of the huge hall, rolling and repeating themselves between pillars and amid the groining of the roof.

"That's the quickest way to bwing them," said Gabriel.

Barry looked inquiring.

"The waiters," explained Gabriel. "That's the fire signal, they never huwwy unless they think the place is on fire. They'll be here at the double, you'll see."

"But why not have them——" began Barry, then stopped.

"Oh, they are not allowed in the Gweat Hall, it's against the wules. Her Majesty likes the place to look like a cathedwal. It can't look like a cathedwal with a lot of waiters loungin' about in it playin' shove-ha'penny, so they stay in their own quarters until they're called."

"Where are their quarters—if I am not asking too many questions? I trust I am not fatiguing you?"

"Indeed, no. Too pleased. Feedin' quarters down below, sleepin' quarters up above."

Barry stared up into the lofty roof, in whose dim height the thunder rolled.

"And how many of them are there?"

"Waiters? I could not swear," drawled Captain Gabriel, dismounting from his horse. "The Wegiment hires them by the hundwed. There's a litttle cemetewy wound the back in the gwounds, somewhere, I believe, where they're burwied from time to time."

"Indeed," murmured Barry, also dismounting. "And are they married? That is, do their wives and children live down below, too?"

"Stwictly forbidden to admit a wife or child to the Club on pain of shootin'. Against the wules, you see. They live wound about, outside. Each man is allowed one dagueweotype, not to include more than thwee members of his family, and is allowed to look at it for thwee and a half minutes a day. That's to keep them from becomin' hardened. The Colonel is not a bwute."

"One sees that," murmured Barry.

"Evwy evenin' at six o'clock Doctor Pwessure conducts Waiters' Pwayers. Jawin' to them about their sins. *And* thwee times on Sundays. Evwy care is taken of their souls. Awful bwevity of our sojurn here, an' all that. All the same, they're a deuced ungwateful webellious discontented lot. Ask Baird, ask anyone. You'll see."

Here the murmur which had been growing louder ever since Gabriel sounded the gong swelled to a roar as a crowd of waiters rushed into the hall, shouting and waving their arms."

"Fire, fire!"

"Where's ve fire, Capting?" asked a waiter who was rather thinner than the rest.

"There is no fire," said Gabriel in the low cold tone he kept for the waiters.

The waiter who had asked the question turned back to his advancing comrades with a gesture of despair, saying in a hoarse voice, "It's no use, mates. We got the Monkey's Allowance again."

There was a low murmur of anger and disappointment, but the men made no further movement. They stood still with resigned expressions on their faces as if awaiting orders.

"Take the horses and water them," commanded Gabriel.

"Vewy good, Capting."

The waiters silently filed out, looking rebellious and secretive.

"I will take you to your wooms, if you are agweeable, Molloy?" said Gabriel, "and then we will dine. New officers always dine in Mess on their first evenin' here."

The word "dine" aroused unpleasant feelings in Barry. He had no money, and did not know when he would receive his first pay. But he decided to say nothing, and to trust to the kindness and tactfulness which he felt sure Captain Gabriel was exerting on his behalf. He was greatly attracted by Captain Gabriel's air of mingled power and mildness; at first he could not recall where he had before seen a countenance expressing exactly those qualities, and yet he was sure, quite sure, that he had seen it. Suddenly, he recollected that an aunt living in London had once sent him a representation of the Nelson Monument, and it was on the countenances of the Lions which everlastingly guard the monument of a grateful nation to its hero that he had seen that very look of indolent power.

The storm had gathered again overhead, thunder rolled up in the roof and once the vast spaces were lit by the glare of lightning. The corridors and halls and closed doors that he could see on all sides were now made mysterious by deepening twilight, and that unmistakable atmosphere of luxury and terror informed the great building which is only encountered in the palace of a tyrant.

A horse-drawn tram now appeared in the distance, running between two pathways of richest crimson pile carpet and driven by a small, sullen waiter. The tram was empty and Gabriel and Barry boarded it.

"The Officers' Quarters," commanded Gabriel curtly, and folding his arms became silent.

Barry was glad of the opportunity to give his full attention to the objects now flitting past in the dimness as the tram gathered speed. Once they passed a chapel where candles burned before an altar with lilies, once he saw a gymnasium where men were drilling with clubs. Frequently they passed bronze statues of noble female figures holding up torches, or cornucopias apparently filled with books; he saw marble staircases covered with rich red or yellow carpets, and giant aspidistra plants many feet high, whose glossy leaves burgeoned from porcelain tubs.

"Twacts," suddenly observed Gabriel.

"I beg your pardon?"

"Those things in those things those old girls are cawwy-in', don't you know," explained Gabriel, jerking his head at a statue, which was already receding into the distance, of a noble woman with a cornucopia. "Her Majesty has them especially designed for the Club. Wouldn't have gwapes or apples. She don't appwove of stwong dwink. Twacts instead. If you climbed up you could wead the titles 'Little Soldiers and Big Battles' and all that sort of stuff."

His tone, though amiable, was melancholy and reserved, and did not encourage Barry to comment upon what he said, so silence fell once more. But the increasing splendour and order of his surroundings, a regimented gorgeousness, a magnificent precision of luxury which irrresistibly suggested that it was designed and executed by a military mind, worked so strongly upon Barry that at last he could keep silent no longer, but observed——

"I suppose that this must be the finest building in London—in the world, for that matter?"

His youthful voice, which was only coloured by a brogue, gave charm to his speech. Gabriel roused himself, stared at him for a second, and then smiled kindly.

"I believe you, my boy! And it costs a mint of money to keep up," he added—rather coarsely, Barry thought. "It's no joke wunning this place, I can tell you."

"But surely the Government . . ." began Barry.

"This is Her Majesty's hobby, not the Government's, and we're wesponsible to her for every bwown we spend."

He paused, and muttered something that Barry did not quite catch about saving the dwipping off the beef.

"She sees the accounts every month," he went on, "and there's no hope of cookin' them, either."

Barry felt eager for more information, but his native caution prevented him from giving expression to his feelings beyond a sympathetic inclination of the head and a slight murmur.

They were now passing rows of doors, each half-concealed by a heavy curtain of violet velvet. When the tram reached a door near the end of the row it stopped, and Gabriel stood up, Barry doing likewise.

"Lieutenant's quarters," said Gabriel, as they alighted.

The little waiter, who was driving, now turned his head in their direction.

"'Ow about waiting, Capting?"

"Certainly," returned Gabriel icily.

"Nearly six o'clock. Time for Waiters' Prayers, Capting."

Gabriel did not answer. His back was turned and he was about to pull a bell-rope of violet silk outside the door.

"Waiters' Prayers, six o'clock," repeated the waiter, putting his head round the side of the tram and slightly raising his voice.

Still Gabriel said nothing. He pulled the bell-rope.

"Oright, then! If I go to 'ell it's all your fort!" screamed the waiter, and burst into a passion of hysterical tears.

Gabriel said, without looking round:

"Your Dagueweotype time is docked by two minutes."

There was a pause. Then the waiter said:

"Very good, Capting."

Barry and Gabriel stepped into the room beyond, the person who had opened the door to them standing respectfully aside to let them pass. Barry had already taken an impression of a long pale countenance, lowered eyelids, and a ginger moustache.

"Badd, your servant," explained Gabriel, going on into the room. Here low settees covered in crimson velvet, shaded lamps hung with beaded covers, glossy cabinets stacked with cigars, and a large and glowing fire conveyed a delightful promise of comfort.

"Come out when you've changed; we dine with the Colonel, as I said. I'll take you along," said Gabriel, dropping his hand for a moment upon the young man's shoulder.

"I will, thank you. You are most kind," said Barry, wishing that he had had his uniform.

"Not at all, my dear fellow. In an hour, then."

Gabriel smiled, gave Barry's shoulder a slight pressure, and went out.

Barry's toilet was made in a hip-bath filled with water

by Badd, who received jug after jug brought to a door in an inner room by a procession of staggering waiters. While Barry was negligently examining the small china wash-basin, adorned by a cluster of seashells in coral and brown, he overheard stifled cries from the passage outside, and these were followed by the noise of a pistol-shot.

"There!" observed one of the waiters in a low voice, as he set down his can of water.

" 'Ow do you mean, *there*?" sneered Badd, in the same subdued tone.

"They've got 'im this time."

Badd was silent. Barry heard the sound of water being poured into the bath. "It's 'ard if a cove can't say 'is prayers," said the waiter presently.

This time Badd answered; his voice was soft and controlled.

"Oo are you to be wanting to say yer prayers, you article?"

"I never sez *I* wanted to say any prayers. I only sez that *if* a cove *should* want to, it's 'ard if he can't."

"Praying ain't encouraged round 'ere."

"Selp my taters it ain't! Unless you prays to You-know-Oo."

"That's enough. Cut it."

Badd came noiselessly out of the bedroom and stood at Barry's side.

"The bath is ready, sir."

Barry did not answer, but unbuttoned his coat and handed it to the man without looking at him. He felt, though he could not see, that Badd's face expressed approval. He was greatly relieved, for his own part, to see a uniform laid out in readiness upon the bed.

When he had bathed, Badd assisted him into the mess-dress of a lieutenant in the Bloods; tight trousers of copper cloth and a jacket of purple velvet decorated with loops of copper braid. He looked at himself in the swing mirror on the wooden stand, with a pleasure that for the life of him he could not have concealed. Badd was busy at the other end of the room; there was no one else to see him in his glory, and suddenly he wished that a girl were standing beside him, to throw her white arms about his neck and tell him he looked a hero.

CHAPTER III

THERE was a knock at the door and Badd went to open it.

Gabriel stood there, superb in the mess-dress of a captain in the Bloods, a greatcoat of dark purple cloth encrusted with rich astrakhan hanging from his mighty shoulders. A large cigar sent aromatic wreaths of smoke into the luxuriance of his beard. He looked Barry over, then gave the briefest of nods.

"Capital. Shall we go up?"

"By all means. I am quite ready." Barry's voice was lower than usual because of his nervousness. Badd gently shut the door behind them.

A small tram drawn by one horse with a knot of coloured ribbons on its head awaited them at some distance away, and they walked towards it.

"A pwivate twam," explained Captain Gabriel. "Officers can hire them if they wish. More comfortable than those wegulation ones. Got hot-water bottles."

While they were arranging themselves in two small seats which had thick rugs attached to them, Barry noticed that the driver of the tram was trying to attract the attention of Gabriel. At the same moment Gabriel himself observed the man's efforts and without looking up from the rug he was buckling about his knees, inquired in a low, chilly tone:

"Well, Licker?"

"It's ve Colonel, Capting."

"Well?"

"'E's at it again, Capting."

"Explain." Gabriel's voice was even quieter; he leant back and folded his arms, without giving the man a glance.

"Wiv ve knives, Capting. You know."

A trace of embarrassment appeared on Gabriel's face. He said quickly, bending as if to examine a mark upon the rug——

"Oh—ah, yes, exactly so. Well, dwive on, man, dwive on, what the deuce are you waiting for?"

The waiter climbed into his seat with a look of sly satisfaction on his pock-marked face, and the tram dashed off.

The storm was coming up again. As they traversed corridor after corridor, without movement or life save for the moonlit clouds scudding past the vast uncurtained windows, Barry heard distant thunder, and intermittently a blaze of lightning silently lit up the heavens. The air was growing colder. The horse was now putting all its strength to pulling the tram up a steep incline. Barry was grateful for the heat of the stone bottle upon his knees.

Far below, huddled and dark, were the roofs of London; chimneys and turrets and spires thrown into goblin prominence against the dreary flare of gaslight from the streets.

"We're goin' up the South Tower," explained Captain Gabriel. "The dinin' hall's up there. Not cold, are you, I twust?"

"No, indeed, I thank you." Barry set his teeth so that they should not chatter.

The single tramline still ascended, and the glass walls on either side grew closer every moment. Suddenly the

glare of gaslight from below and the light of the moon
from above were alike obscured, and the tram moved on
in a dismal dimness illuminated by occasional flashes of
lightning.

"A cloud," observed Gabriel, inclining his head towards
the white mist rolling against the glass walls. "We are
almost at our destination."

A moment more, and the tram stopped at a small platform covered with a rich Indian carpet. Above, the roof
was hidden in deep shadows. Immediately opposite was
a door sheathed in copper.

"Here we are," said Gabriel, standing up and giving his
mighty shoulders a shake. "Wait," he added to the
driver.

"Cold up 'ere," said the man impudently.

"Natuwally. Wap the wugs wound yourself. That is an
order. We do not wequire anyone to fweeze themselves
to death or cweate any twouble of that sort. Come, my
dear Molloy."

He pulled a rope outside the door, and then they stood
side by side on the platform, where there was barely room
for them, waiting.

The cloud still drifted past, hiding the glow from the
city; the only light was the softened red ray from a lamp
above their heads, made of ruby glass and pierced Oriental
work.

Suddenly the doors slid apart, and Barry found himself
on the threshold of a large circular hall.

Light poured from an enormous chandelier, in whose
glittering drops sprang tiny beams of coloured fire, and
all round the walls (which were hung with white and red
striped satin) were ranged some twenty sconces, each
carrying forty candles. The radiance was soft, yet
dazzling; the floor was covered by a rich red Aubusson
carpet massed with lighter roses and loops of green
ribbon; the chairs and long table were of massive and

glowing mahogany from the forests of Burma; yet the roof above all this splendour was a glass and metal framework through which the night sky was visible; and even as Barry glanced up, the lightning blazed again.

The room was very silent. But it was not empty of human life.

At one end of the long table was sitting a group of seven or eight gentlemen in the regimental mess attire, so close together that they might without unfairness have been described as huddling. Some were twisting the stems of their glasses; others staring in silence at the shining board; others were gazing, as if fascinated, at the solitary figure seated at the far end of the table.

This was a man in full patrols, whose epaulettes of copper lace smouldered in the light from the chandelier. His arms were folded and his head proudly lifted as if to meet a challenge. In front of him was a pile of table knives; a mass of glittering steel that also reflected the candlelight.

Some epergnes of purple glass filled with nuts and grapes and the port, which had evidently been passing round, completed the furnishings of the table.

Barry glanced at Gabriel. His face was expressionless; he looked almost asleep. It was evident that he would give no explanation. Barry transferred his gaze to the scene before him. The silence remained unbroken.

Suddenly a change came over the moving white ceiling that was a cloud; the last shreds of mist were drifting past, revealing the night sky. At the same instant a flash of lightning fell into the banqueting hall. A thousand dazzling rays sprang from the knives; blue flames ran down the blades and died away at the ends of their handles while a quivering luminosity played about the heap and enveloped the head and shoulders of the gentleman with the epaulettes, who sat motionless, with folded arms, amid the eerie radiance.

A tremendous clap of thunder followed, shaking the tower and striking elfin tinklings from the chandelier.

The officers at the other end of the table seemed to shrink closer to each other. In the silence following the thunderclap, Gabriel strode across and took his seat among them. Barry did not know if he were supposed to do so, but he followed.

No one spoke. One of the gentlemen, a handsome boy with curly hair, tried to crack a walnut but the instrument fell from his hand to the table, with a loud clatter. All the gentlemen sprang some inches in the air and subsided again. Barry caught subdued oaths, and fierce glances were directed at the youthful officer, but no one said anything. He was exceedingly hungry but forgot his faintness in the interest of the scene before him.

Again the lightning leapt into the hall; again the heap of knives blazed with awesome fire; again the thunder crashed and all the officers huddled a little closer together. The figure at the head of the table never moved.

When the echoes had died away, Barry became aware that whispering was going on all about him:

"Go on, Milde, my dear fellow."

"But it is not my turn, I assure you."

"Cussett, then?"

"Not for worlds, dear boy."

"Gabriel, will you not go? By Jove, we shall get no play if this continues!"

The last speaker was a handsome man with greying hair, in the prime of the late forties. Barry was studying him with interest when, to his dismay, the gentleman's eyes met his own. Leaning forward he exclaimed in an imperious whisper:

"You, sir! Molloy, I presume. You will go, will you not?"

Everyone looked at Barry. His mouth was dry and his heart beating hard as he answered in what he tried to make a composed whisper:

"Of course, sir."

"Capital!"

"Excellent!"

"Eureka!"

The excited whispers sounded all round him.

But when they had ceased to sound, there was silence. He looked from one face to another, but all wore the same expression of eager interest mingled with excitement; and no one spoke.

It was plain that the officers wanted to leave the table but etiquette forbade them to do so while the gentleman sat there in front of his dinner knives. Therefore the gentleman must be induced to get up. Right!

There was no time to think. He must make his plans while he advanced towards that figure at the head of the table. He turned quickly away from the eager faces and began to walk, not too fast and not too slowly, down the room.

CHAPTER IV

NOW only a few feet of brilliantly illuminated air separated him from that rigid and splendid form, and he could see round the other side of the pile of table-knives. Immediately in front of the Colonel was a plate of macaroni cheese and a large hand-mirror reflecting his face.

Barry halted. He flexed one knee, leant a little forward, and said in a respectful yet urgent whisper:

"Sir . . . your eyes!"

There was a pause. Mist seemed to float before his own eyes. The room was completely silent, and ages passed.

Then he became aware that the Colonel's head was slowly turning in his direction. Dark emotional orbs were fixed doubtfully upon his own.

"Your eyes, sir!" he repeated quickly. "Lightning has a most injurious effect upon the human eye. A cousin of mine lost the power to focus by the action of lightning."

For a moment the Colonel continued to look at him uncertainly. Then he slowly unfolded his arms and relaxed. At once Barry heard the sound of chairs being pushed back, and there was a commotion overhead; someone had pulled the cords that drew a curtain of silver satin over the ceiling. A second later, Captain Gabriel had him by the arm and was presenting him to the Colonel.

"Lieutenant Molloy, sir. Awwived this afternoon fwom Ireland."

"I am happy to welcome you," said the Colonel languidly, inclining his head; he seemed exhausted.

"Thank you, sir."

"You are sensible, no doubt, of the honour attaching to a commission in this regiment."

"Most sensible, indeed, sir."

"In your behaviour, appearance and progress nothing will be accepted that falls short of perfection."

"I understand, sir."

"No dull boots."

"Of course, sir."

"Nor frayed ends."

"No, sir."

"Or brooding or grubby gloves or *idling*!" On the last word the Colonel's voice rose to a musical roar. At the same time he glanced impatiently round, and beckoned to a small officer with scanty whiskers, who at once hurried forward. "The men are shockingly idle," went on the Colonel, "they spend far too much time at night in sleeping. Major Milde!"

"Sir?"

"You may accompany me downstairs and play the harp to me."

"You are too good, sir," responded Major Milde, hastily assuming an expression of rapture.

"I know what a treat music is to you, my dear fellow. But you must put out your cigar, you know," and the Colonel playfully flipped it out of Major Milde's hand; it fell on the floor, where Captain Gabriel, in moving backwards, inadvertently trod upon it. "You do not need cigars, you will exhaust your faculties before your time. You are a sad fellow, indeed, with your cigars! Now come, we shall have three full hours of music before Lights Out."

The officers stood at attention while the Colonel, who was taller than Captain Gabriel but not so broad, strode out of the room accompanied by Major Milde.

When the door had closed upon them Major Baird clapped Barry on the back.

"Well done, Molloy!"

"A bang-up attack, by George!"

"What did you say to him?"

Barry repeated his remarks to the Colonel, which were received with approval, but the subject was immediately dropped; and he gathered that they were all anxious not to discuss the matter.

He was introduced to Ensign Cussett, the young man who had dropped the nut-crackers, and to a gay-faced youth with dark whiskers named Ensign Dannit. These, with Major Baird and the absent Milde, made up the group that had been sitting about the table.

When the introductions were over, Gabriel observed:

"You must be wavenous. We are going to play, but do you addwess yourself to your wepast. Perhaps you will join us later."

A waiter now appeared, apparently from a door concealed behind the wall draperies, and while Major Baird and the rest gathered about a blazing fire, a place was set for Barry at the table, and the Colonel's plate and the hand-mirror were carried away.

Barry was glad to address himself to some exquisite soup, followed by some salmon, and was beginning to feel both rested and in rising spirits as he sat there eating and drinking, and watching, without appearing to do so, the group gathered about the card-table.

He was observing the progress of the waiters, who were busy at a side table with a large silver dish, when one of them uttered a low cry.

"Cor stone me up a gum tree!"

The group at the card-table did not turn round, but Major Baird got slowly up and strolled across the room. The waiters were bending over the silver dish, gesticulating and muttering.

"What is the matter?" inquired Major Baird in a chill tone, looking at the ash on the end of his cigar.

"It's a-gorn, sir," said a waiter who, without being fat, was less starveling than the others and seemed much distressed. "As nice a bird as ever come out of Smithfield. Look, sir. Gorn between 'ere and the kitchen."

Barry, peering between the forms of the waiters, could see that the silver dish, save for some watercress and a little gravy, was empty. But there seemed to be white paper or card, where a bird should have been.

Major Baird bending over this, started back and exclaimed in a low voice:

"The Wolf!"

All the waiters nodded, and a moan came from the group, which Major Baird immediately checked with a wave of his cigar.

"That will do. Get another bird immediately. I will explain to Lieutenant Molloy. Hurry!"

The waiters scurried away, apparently in agitation and distress, but Barry, watching them vanish through the draperies, saw one of them glance back towards the silver dish with an expression of delight.

He was still puzzling over this when Major Baird approached and seated himself easily upon the edge of the table.

"I am sorry to say there will be a slight delay before the next course," he said, smiling down at Barry. "You have been the victim of The Wolf. He has stolen your woodcock."

"The Wolf?" repeated Barry.

The Major blew out some smoke.

"Ay, the Wolf. None of us know anything of him, save that he is a gallant and daring soldier. While we were campaigning in India last year he brought in two dacoits one evening, trussed like fowls, ha, ha! We found 'em in the dust of the compound. It was he who captured Punna Singh, known more familiarly as the Monster of Meerut, also the Demon of Delhi, the Pest of Peshaur, the Curse of Calcutta, the Besom of Bombay and the Bad Luck of Lucknow——"

"They are all names, I take it, of the same infidel and treacherous ruler?"

"Oh, no; they are—or were, for they are no longer alive, I am happy to say—as wicked a crew of heathen dogs as ever polluted the burning sands of India."

"And the mysterious unknown captured them all?"

Major Baird smilingly nodded.

"Single-handed?"

"We do not know. But we suspect so. They were delivered, with the mail from home, outside the barracks. One every three months throughout the campaign.

"Indeed," said Barry.

"Trussed like fowls, ha, ha! every man jack of 'em."

"You amaze me."

"I assure you that we were amazed ourselves. In the face of such daring you may imagine we are disposed to overlook small escapades such as the stealing of a wood-cock now and then, or the loss of all the pillows off our beds on a winter night."

"And you have no idea who he is?" cried Barry.

"None."

Barry was silent for a moment. It occurred to him that he had perhaps betrayed too much interest and excitement in The Wolf; both emotions were unsuited to a gentleman and a swell. When he spoke again his voice was calmer.

"No doubt he has his reasons for remaining anony-mous."

"No doubt. And while his actions redound to the credit of the Regiment we shall respect them."

It crossed Barry's mind that the stealing of someone's dinner was hardly an action that redounded to the credit of the Regiment but he suppressed the thought.

"Oh, The Wolf is a wonderful fellow!" said Major Baird ardently, getting up from the table as a waiter approached, carrying another silver dish. "But I must not keep you from your woodcock," and he smiled and strolled back to the card-table.

Thither, after he had finished a superb meal with Turkish coffee and a few puffs at a narghile (a novelty to him), Barry also repaired; and the remainder of the evening passed in play.

But there was a shadow upon the night's enjoyment. He lost four pounds nineteen shillings and sixpence to Captain Gabriel and, all penniless as he was, laughingly promised to pay him on the morrow.

As the gentlemen wrapped themselves into their rugs in the private trams, he was wondering how the deuce he was going to find the money.

It was cold and still on the downward journey. The storm had passed and the sky was full of summer stars, steady and cold. London slept, save for the hellish glow here and there that marked a gin palace or the dim light burning above a bed of sickness. The great building was silent; lamps burned unwaveringly and the air was redolent of cigar smoke and hot-house flowers.

"Good night, my dear fellow," said Gabriel, leaning from his tram to shake hands with Barry as the *cortège* paused outside the latter's door. "I twust your first day with us has been a pleasant one?"

"It has, indeed . . . thanks to your kindness," returned Barry, moved, despite his cautiousness, by the other's manner.

"Tush, my dear fellow. Delighted. Good night to you, then. We shall meet to-morrow at the parwade."

His tram hastened away, in the wake of the others, and Barry let himself into his chambers.

CHAPTER V

BADD was sitting upright in a chair beside the fire reading a little book with a picture of a large bat and an unclothed female on the cover. He stood smartly to attention as Barry entered and saluted.

"I will go to bed at once, Badd."

"Very good, Lieutenant." He began to help Barry off with his jacket. "This here come for you, sir," and he held out a letter.

Barry took it in some surprise, hoping that it was not a bill, and opened it.

DEAR MOLLOY,

Would you like to borrow five pounds? Pray do not think me intrusive, but I know that one's first evening in the Regiment is often spoiled by worrying about money. My own was. If you would like five pounds, pray let Badd know, and he will bring it to you with your morning tea. I hope we shall soon have the pleasure of meeting.

In pleasant anticipation,

GERARD TOLOREAUX.

Barry read this with growing anger. Who was the fellow? A moneylending tout? He tossed it on the bed, and presently, while buttoning the neck of his frilled nightshirt, inquired coldly:

"Who is that from?"

"Looks like Lieutenant Toloreaux's writin', sir. Didn't you meet 'im to-night?"

Barry shook his head.

"Very playful gent, sir. Not quite right in the 'ead, some of the gents say."

"Indeed."

"Ticky, the other officers calls him."

"Why is that?"

"Couldn't rightly say, sir."

Barry was silent, as he lay with his head upon the deep soft pillow. He was deeply angered. Who had betrayed his poverty and exposed him to this impertinent jest? How had Lieutenant Toloreaux guessed his need for five pounds?

"Sorry to 'ear you was unlucky at the cards to-night, sir," observed Badd, who was folding up his clothes.

"Who told you I was unlucky?"

"Things gets round, sir. Will you be wantin' me any more to-night, sir?"

"No. You can get out."

"Very good, sir. Good night, sir."

Barry did not answer. Badd extinguished the lamps, leaving the room in the light of the dying fire, and went softly away.

· · · · ·

Agneo Testetti, an Italian waiter, who had come to

England in exile with the Rossettis and drifted into slavery at the Club from lack of means, had still had some spirit left, five years ago.

In one of his mad fits, shouting an old war song he had first heard sung by The Thousand marching with Garibaldi, he had climbed up the lofty entrance to the Waiters' Quarters and scrawled in black paint:

Lasciate ogni speranza voi chi entrate.

Another waiter, with some remnants of education left (he had once been a servitor at Radley College) had written a translation underneath in red paint:

All hope abandon, ye who enter here.

And a third waiter, a once-clean little man from the country, had crossed out "Hope" and written "Soap" over it, in bright yellow lettering.

The inscription, therefore, which immediately met the eye above the Waiters' Quarters, was:

All Soap abandon, ye who enter here.

It was deadly cold up in the North Tower where the waiters slept. The rotten wooden bunks were attached to the metal and glass framework, and when the snow fell there was nothing between them and it but a sheet of glass. The little ladders leading up to the bunks were sheathed in ice. Waiters frequently slipped down them and broke their legs. No one in authority took any notice, so they doctored one another. Incapable of organization, co-operation and rationalization as they were, they yet showed a foolish kindness towards one another, unsupported by reason and unrewarded by results.

The rags in which the waiters slept were foul with grease and age, and a mixture of dust and frost coated the wooden bunks. The glass was yellow with fog and fume from the clouds. As their wives were not allowed up there, no duster or mop or pail had ever appeared on the scene, and the only homely touch was the daguerreotypes; rows and rows of them, yellowed with age and curling with damp, pasted or pinned above the bunks. Each had its faded insciption: "Me and my dear wife on our wedding day," "My Emily," "Me and her," "Her and me, 1840," "Her," "Them." In many cases there was no mark but a cross, a childish kiss scrawled upon the hem of a crinoline or over a pair of little boots.

These daguerreotypes were not supposed to be visible, as the waiters were only allowed to look at them for three and a half minutes a day each; so they were covered by narrow curtains that could be pulled aside by a cord. But as each waiter was bound, by custom, to have his three and a half minutes a day, all the waiters had put their daguerreotype time together and found that it added up to twenty-four hours. By taking their time in strict rotation, therefore, they argued that the daguerreotypes could all remain uncovered all the time. This satisfied their logic, though it would scarcely have satisfied anyone else's, and as no one, except an occasional private soldier, ever ventured up the tower to see if orders were carried out (it was taken for granted that they were) the daguerreotypes remained uncovered for all to feast upon.

A small brazier burned upon the platform round which arose the tiers of bunks, and on this night all the waiters were gathered about it. Only a few could get close, but even those seated upon the edge of the bunks higher up could inhale a little of the delicious and unfamiliar warmth, as it floated upwards.

And to-night, as they huddled about the coals or leant forward into the flamelight from fifty feet overhead, their shadows thrown weirdly upon the dull glass of the roof, whom were they toasting? Whose name did they cry aloud, but softly, lest the gentlemen sleeping far below should hear them through their dreams?

And what was Arthur Sobber lifting from the coals, savoury and dripping with gravy, ready to be cut into shreds; a shred for each famished man? A woodcock!

"The Wolf!" they cried, again and again, their voices falling eerily down into the darkness. "God bless 'im! The Wolf!"

CHAPTER VI

AT nine o'clock the next morning Doctor Harrovius Pressure, Headmaster of the First Bloods' Military Preparatory School, was in his study, praying.

He was kneeling on a little cushion embroidered with a glass of wine in red silk. This had been worked for him by a young person whom he had known many years ago. He now knelt upon it for two reasons: to wear it out so that it should *not* remind him of a time when he had been a deadly sinner, and at the same time to remind him of that period, in order that he should not be too pleased with himself now. But it was taking a long time to wear out, because the young person had used strong embroidery silk in a very bright red.

We are sorry to say that at one time Doctor Pressure had passed the nights with this young person, and the days in correcting her grammar, for she had not been a lady. Once, on the occasion of his birthday, she had presented him with this little cushion in memory of the one bottle of wine he had ever bought her, and of the evening they had spent together in drinking it (that is, in drinking half of it, for at ten o'clock Doctor Pressure had suddenly realized how wicked they were being and had poured the rest of the wine away).

In spite of this abrupt conclusion to their feast, the young person had looked back upon this evening with tenderness, as being the only one upon which Doctor Pressure had forgotten, under the baneful influence of the grape, to tell her not to say, "I done" and "ain't," and of these tender memories the little cushion was the fruit.

Doctor Pressure prayed with his face hidden in his hands and bits of his long black and grey beard sticking out through his fingers.

He had just got to the kinder bit he always put at the end of his prayers, asking God, after crushing the boys, to make them sorry for their sins, when he had to conclude his devotions more abruptly than was his wont, because someone was knocking at the door of his study.

"Come in, come in," called Doctor Pressure, getting up from the little cushion and hastily stuffing it into a special drawer painted with sorrowful black paint. Then he sat down at his desk, facing the door, with a severe yet kindly smile.

The door opened and a youth of some fifteen summers stood timidly regarding him.

"Come in, George Licker," said the Doctor amiably. "You have interrupted me at my devotions, but let us forget that. What is it, my boy, that brings you here at this time? You should be mashing the acorns for the boys' midday meal."

"I have done so, sir," answered the boy, while a bright smile illuminated his fresh and rosy face. He was neatly dressed in a shabby but clean suit and his hands were newly washed.

"You know I would not have come, sir, if it hadn't been something important." As George Licker spoke, the brightness slowly faded from his face and he grew pale.

"I know it, indeed, my boy," replied the Doctor gravely. "What is amiss? Come in. Shut the door. Sit down. So. Now. What ails you?"

George was looking at the floor and slowly twisting his hands together. He was in so much distress that he could not speak.

"Come, my boy," said the Doctor without impatience. "You know that whatever you have to tell me will be kept secret between us; secret, that is, if no one else is injured in any way by its being kept secret. Of course, if it concerns in any way the honour of the School or the prestige of the Regiment," and the Doctor's voice grew stern, "then it must be revealed to those in authority, terrible though the consequences may be."

"Oh, sir," muttered George, who was now weeping into a very clean handkerchief, "it *does* concern the School and the Regiment. But——"

"But what, my boy?"

"But it is too horrible for me to tell you in words. May I ask you to be so good, sir, as to come and see the goings-on for yourself?"

"By all means I will come," said the Doctor, gravely yet vigorously, rising from his chair and settling his gown and taking from a table his mortar-board and putting it upon his head. "Lead the way."

They left the study and went along a corridor which led into the extensive grounds surrounding the school. Their progress across the lawns was unimpeded. A platoon was being drilled in the square but otherwise they met no one.

At last they came—oh, horror! what was about to be revealed? the Doctor started back and put his hand across his eyes for a moment in prayer—to the Chapel, the pride of the Military School.

It had stained-glass windows designed by Mr. Burne-Jones, and paid for with the money subscribed by the African Savages and Slaves Association, in the delusion that they were thus purchasing the right to have their portraits in the Great White Queen's Ju-Ju House; and that their bodies would shortly be magically transported thither also, and they would then be free. And it was true that Mr. Burne-Jones *had* put some Africans into the stained-glass windows: two of them stood behind the chair of General Ramm, founder of the Regiment, the Club and the Military School, fanning the General as he sat in his chair with his foot on the neck of a heathen.

Quietly the Doctor and George Licker approached the sacred edifice. A matutinal hush lay over the gardens, made more pleasant by the occasional sweet song of a bird.

George Licker reverently opened the door of the chapel, and stood aside to let Doctor Pressure enter.

The Doctor swept into the sacred edifice with a rustle of his gown, snatching the mortar-board from his head and bowing reverently as he did so, but at the same time darting sharp glances from under his heavy eyebrows to see what was toward.

The sight that met his gaze was so appalling, so hideous, that he started back, dropping his mortar-board, and uttered a low and disbelieving cry of:

"No, no!"

A large object, presumably a human being, though it was not possible to say so with decision, was jumping backwards and forwards across the pews. Neither was it possible to discern the sex of this object, because it was wrapped from head to foot in the Union Jack.

In the silence, unbroken save for the painful breathing of the Doctor and the eager breathing of George Licker, a song could be heard proceeding from the muffled figure:

> My mother *said*
> I never *should*
> Play with the *gip*sies
> In the *wood*.
> If I did
> She would *say*
> Naughty boy
> To run aw*ay*.

The figure timed its jumps to the words of the rhyme, landing with a soft thud on each word which it emphasized.

Doctor Pressure advanced. As the figure landed immediately in front of him, he reached out and snatched off the Union Jack.

A slight rosy young man in the early twenties stood there, regarding him with an amiable expression.

"Lieutenant Toloreaux!" exclaimed the Doctor.

The young man saluted.

"Come outside, sir, come outside," said the Doctor in an agitated whisper. "We cannot discuss this matter in the sacred edifice. Come outside at once."

Lieutenant Toloreaux obediently followed the Doctor along the aisle and out through the door into the porch, where George Licker was standing, looking pale and distressed.

"You may go, George Licker," said the Doctor gravely. "Remember you are put upon your honour to say no word of this matter to your humble companions in the Waiters' Quarters."

"Oh, sir!" muttered George. "Cannot I hope that you can trust me?"

"I know I can, my dear boy," returned the Doctor, turning up the corners of his mouth and screwing up his eyes in a grave sweet smile. "Go now; you should be stewing the beechmast for the boys' pudding."

During this conversation Lieutenant Toloreaux had stood in silence. Now, as the Doctor drew a deep breath and turned to him, he suddenly sat down on the grass.

"Get up, sir!" thundered the Doctor.

"Oh, come, Doctor! It is much more pleasant sitting on the grass."

"Pleasant, sir! Pleasant! You dare to use the word to me, when you should be lying prostrate before the altar in the sacred edifice you have profaned, weeping in penitence and racked with remorse. Consider, sir, your work upon this morning. First, you have deeply wounded a sensitive and chivalrous boy. Next, you have drawn me forth from my studies upon an errand that has riven me to the depths of my soul with the extreme of horror. Thirdly, sir, you have desecrated the altar of your God and, finally, you have outraged and insulted the Flag— that Flag which (were you a human being, which I am inclined, sir, to doubt) should be sacred to you as the prayers taught you at your mother's knee."

"Well, I'm deuced sorry you caught me at it, I must say," observed Lieutenant Toloreaux with feeling.

"I do not wish to hear of your sorrow, sir. I intend to go deeper than that. I intend to have the matter fully explained. I intend to force you to confess why you should engage in such a hideous prank, a prank which must cause all right-minded men to shudder."

"I knew you would," said the young man, gazing at the angry doctor towering above him.

"Have no fear, sir. As you well know, I have no authority over you. I shall refer you to your Colonel. He will know how to deal with you. No. I do not even desire to punish you. My province, sir, is the spiritual, not the military. You must answer to the Colonel for your body, to me for your soul. Now, sir," and here the Doctor's voice began to soften to a manly and winning note, "will you not put your hard-heartedness away, and rise up and look me in the eyes and tell me *why* you did this dreadful thing?"

"Well, I suppose I had best do so," said Lieutenant Toloreaux at last, "but *pray* do sit down, Doctor Pressure, I can speak better so."

After a struggle with himself and a brief prayer with his hand over his eyes, Doctor Pressure said:

"Well, I will sit down if you wish. I have little or no spiritual pride, I thank God. I will sit upon His grass as readily with a sinner as with a saint. If it will help you to ease your soul of this dreadful sin I will most certainly sit beside you," and he lowered himself carefully down, until he was seated facing Lieutenant Toloreaux.

"I was alone in my chamber early this morning," began the young man, "studying the military strategy of General Ramm when, suddenly, a temptation overcame me, don't you know."

"What was it?" asked the Doctor, eagerly bending towards him.

"To wrap myself in the Flag and jump backwards and forwards over the pews in the chapel, reciting 'My mother said.'"

"Horrible, horrible!" murmured Doctor Pressure, covering his eyes.

"I wrestled with it for some time," continued the young man, speaking more rapidly, "but it overcame me. As though possessed by some sort of an evil spirit, don't you know, I crept down the stairs, prigged—er—obtained the Flag from its position in the chapel, wrapped myself in it and, after one or two failures, succeeded in leaping backwards and forwards over the pews reciting 'My mother said.'"

The Doctor, too overcome to speak, shook his head in silence, keeping his hand over his eyes.

"As I leaped higher, I began to enjoy it, don't you know," continued Lieutenant Toloreaux, his eyes fixed dreamily upon the gate at the far end of the gardens, through which he apparently failed to notice the entire Regiment, headed by the Colonel, now steadily advancing towards them. "'Pon my word, I forgot where I was. I was engaged in wondering whether I could vary the rhyme to 'Up and Down the City Road' when you entered."

Without removing his hand, Doctor Pressure shook his head, muttering, "Vile, vile."

"I cannot hope to convey to you my sensations," con-

tinued the young man, now busily making a daisy-chain.
The Colonel had observed the two gentlemen seated upon
the grass and was making convulsive gestures. Some
officers were spurring their horses forward.

"Do not try, sir," said Doctor Pressure austerely, from
behind the hand. "I am content to let them, as I am
content to let many others, remain a sealed book to me."

"And now here we are," went on Lieutenant Toloreaux
—"sitting side by side like men and brothers, don't you
know, and—and—oh, by Jove! here's the whole Regiment
on top of us!" he ended in dismay.

It was indeed so. Absorbed in his narration it seemed
that he had not observed the cavalcade approaching, and
now they were enclosed on all sides by a silent circle of
very large men seated upon very large horses.

The Colonel, Major Baird and another officer with a
large purple face and a black cow-lick across his brow,
were sitting immediately above them looking down upon
them.

"Doctor Pressure," said the Colonel in a low voice full
of feeling, "what is the meaning of this?"

Doctor Pressure replied in a grave and composed
tone:

"I am speaking with Lieutenant Toloreaux about a
matter that concerns his soul, Colonel."

"His soul, sir, his soul! No man in the regiment has a
soul beyond his duty to it and to me. And it matters to
me, sir, and very much"—here the Colonel's voice rose
to its musical roar—"that one of my officers and the
headmaster of the Military School should be sitting on the
Flag"—here the Colonel saluted, as did all the officers
within earshot—"in broad daylight!"

Doctor Pressure and Lieutenant Toloreaux sprang to
their feet with cries of horror. It was only too true.
Lieutenant Toloreaux, apparently absentmindedly, had
thrown the Flag down upon the grass and seated himself

upon it, and the Doctor was so eager to hear about sin that he, never noticing, had done likewise.

"Oh, I say," muttered Lieutenant Toloreaux agonizedly, going even redder than usual, while Doctor Pressure clenched his fists, bowed his head and blew through his beard to express shame and sorrow.

"Deliberate attempt to foment Radicalism and Chartism among the waiters!" screamed the Colonel.

Dr. Pressure shook his head.

"A terrible oversight. Not deliberate," he muttered hoarsely.

"Oh, I say, sir, you can't think we'd do such a ghastly act on purpose," murmured Lieutenant Toloreaux. "One thing to jump over pews in the Flag, quite another to sit on it. Ungentlemanly."

Barry, who was observing him suspiciously, decided that he was not so distressed as he appeared to be.

"You are evidently raving, Lieutenant Toloreaux," said the Colonel coldly. "What have pews to do with it?"

"Nothing, indeed, sir."

"Cussett, Dannit, take the Flag back into the chapel immediately," went on the Colonel. The two young men saluted, dismounted, and did as they were told. "You, sir," to Doctor Pressure, who was standing with bowed head and mortar-board in hand, "get back to your Virgil and what-do-you-callums. Come now, be off, and do not let this happen again."

Doctor Pressure was here observed to start, and mutter, "Whatdoyoucallums, indeed!" but made no other sign of his resentment than by clapping his hat very hard upon his head and striding off without a backward glance, the tails of his gown fluttering behind him as he went.

"And you, sir, mount at once, and give what little mind the Almighty has bestowed upon you to your military duties. Gentlemen, fall in!"

At a word from Captain Gabriel, Barry, who had been leading a rather old horse with a shabby saddle upon him, rode up to Lieutenant Toloreaux. He had not forgotten the impertinent letter of the night before. "My name is Molloy," he began, looking steadily at the young man.

"How do you do. Delighted to make your acquaintance," said Lieutenant Toloreaux, mounting the old horse and settling himself in the saddle. Barry paid no more attention to him, as they rejoined the main body of the regiment, than to observe that he had but an indifferent seat: and soon the activities of the parade separated them.

CHAPTER VII

THE exercises performed during the parade were severe and prolonged. It was not until one o'clock that the Colonel gave the order "Dis-miss!" and Barry feeling exhausted, yet exhilarated, rode away with Gabriel towards the officers' quarters.

"The afternoon," observed Gabriel, "is fwee."

"Indeed?"

"I take it you would pwefer to spend it alone, explorwin' the gwounds and all that?"

"You are most considerate. I think I should."

"Capital."

They were riding past the preparatory school as Gabriel spoke, and at that moment a lady came out of the cloisters into the sunlight, and stood there, shading her eyes with her hand and looking across the courtyard.

Captain Gabriel reined in his horse, and saluted.

"Er—good afternoon, Miss Beatwice," he said, colouring deeply.

"Oh! Good afternoon, Captain Venner," answered the lady, in whose face Barry observed a similar change.

"Capital day, what?"

"Charming, indeed."

"Just the weather for a dwive."

She was silent, her large blue eyes looking up at him pleadingly from the shade of a white bonnet.

"I was wondewin'," pursued Captain Gabriel resolutely, "if you would care to come for a dwive with me and my aunt, Lady Venner, and Lieutenant Molloy here? May I pwesent him?"

The lady slightly inclined her head and introductions were made. Barry was pleased to increase his circle of respectable acquaintances, but he could not greatly admire Miss Pressure's looks, which were childish rather than striking.

"And—and the dwive?" went on Gabriel after the bows were over. "Will you permit the cawwiage to call for you here at thwee o'clock? With—with my aunt in it, of course," he added, in a tone eager and yet strangely hopeless.

Miss Pressure locked her hands in front of her, and held them steadily there while she shook her head.

"I regret so much . . ." she said faintly, "but it is not possible. I—I must accompany my dear papa to the museum this afternoon."

Gabriel said nothing for a moment. The warm summer breeze swept the dust across the courtyard and fluttered the ribbons on his shoulder-knot. He sat upright on his horse, staring straight in front of him. At last he said gently:

"I too wegwet . . . it is such a charmin' day . . . would have been so pleasant."

"It is the notes for the History of Weapons," said Miss Pressure, in so faint a voice that it came from the inside of her bonnet like the far-off murmur of the sea heard in a large white shell. "We are now doing Knives."

"Knives?"

She bent her head and nodded.

"And—and that means a very great deal of work, you must understand, for everybody all over the world has knives."

Gabriel was listening with his sad eyes fixed upon her face; but Barry thought that he was not hearing the words; he was only hearing the murmur of her voice.

"It was different with Rifles. Only the civilized races have rifles. Then my time—my dear papa's time—was not so fully occupied."

"But I seem to wecollect," said Gabriel gently, "that Doctor Pwessure took notes on Wifles and Darts together."

She bowed her head again, colouring.

"And that your time was as fully occupied then as now."

"It did not seem so to me," she answered. "My dear papa is deriving more satisfaction from Knives than from Rifles. The—the material is more interesting and therefore he is taking more copious notes."

There was another silence. Breaking it, a bell suddenly began to toll loudly. Miss Pressure retreated into the shadow of the cloisters as a crowd of wolfish boys rushed past, silent with hunger, their fierce eyes fixed upon the dining-hall door.

Gabriel drew himself up and saluted and Barry did likewise.

"I wegwet exceedingly that we cannot have the pleasure of your company, Miss Beatwice."

"I too regret it, Captain Venner."

"May I hope that at some other time——?"

"I trust so; but from Knives we shall go on to Missiles,

which includes stones, catapults, bricks. . . . There is a long list and I fear . . ."

"Nevertheless, I may hope?"

She bowed her head for the last time, and walked gracefully down the cloisters as the two gentlemen trotted their horses away. Not once had she smiled.

"You dine alone in your chambers unless summoned to dine in the Mess," said Gabriel as they were dismounting. His pallor and the compression of his lips forbade Barry to comment upon what had just passed.

"I understand."

"We shall meet this evening at Mess. Good day to you," and Gabriel, with a courteous but absent smile, strode off across the now deserted courtyard.

.   .   .   .   .

After a delicious luncheon, served by Badd and two waiters, Barry sat at the open windows of his room with a cigar and *The Clipper*. The view was over an expanse of unmown grass leading to a thick coppice, which shut in this part of the building.

Barry skimmed the pages of *The Clipper*, pulled at his cigar, and now and then glanced idly at the coppice, whose trees wore the heavy green of late summer.

There was a clear jingle of spurs; and Badd stood respectfully before him.

"Yes, what is it?" Barry did not look up.

"It's me afternoon off, please, Lieutenant."

"Very well, you may go."

"Will you be wanting me back to get your tea, sir?"

"I don't know." Barry threw down *The Clipper*, stretched out his arms, and yawned. "No, I think not. I may go out. What's over there?" nodding towards the coppice.

"That, sir? There's the wood, sir, and then there's the place where they bury them articles—the waiters, sir—and a sort o' spa where they has their drink and slops for their womenfolk. Sort of a pleasure gardens, I s'pose they call it."

Barry looked up. Badd was in a gorgeous walking-out dress of closely fitting dark copper cloth with dull gold braid striped down the leg and arm. His cap, adorned with a bunch of purple ribbons, sat on the side of his head.

"Do the officers ever go there?"

"Jus' once, usually, sir. Out o' curiosity."

"Very well. That will do. You may go."

Badd saluted.

Barry, as he looked at him, suddenly smiled. It was a beautiful day, he was full of good lunch, and there seemed not a thing in the world (beyond the rules he had freely taken upon himself as a soldier) to hold him back from adventure and pleasure.

A faint, cautious smile came over Badd's pasty face in return.

"Going to enjoy yourself, Badd?"

"Yes, sir. Me and my sister Bella, sir, and a young person as Bella knows, and a gentleman of my acquaintance, we're all off to 'ave snake-tarts for tea at Wapping."

"Delightful." Barry picked up *The Clipper* once more, disdaining to ask what a snake-tart was.

"Bella's the one." Badd went on, looking at the ground. "She's a starter, Bella is. And a stayer, too. Barmaid at The Bugle Blast just outside the gates 'ere."

"Indeed." Barry was again glancing through the pages of his paper.

"Yes." Suddenly there was feeling in Badd's voice. "Me and Bella, we grew up together. Well—I'm off, sir. Good arternoon."

Barry did not reply, and Badd saluted, went out, and shut the door.

Presently the clock struck three. Barry got up, put on the tasselled cap that completed the walking-out dress he had changed into before lunch, and went out.

The long corridor was deserted. Bright afternoon light poured through the windows and glowed on the crimson carpet bordering the tramlines, the bronze statues, the porcelain tubs now filled with purple begonias. Silence, broken only by the distant hum of the city outside the windows, filled the vast building.

Barry waited by a tram-stop for some five minutes, but as no tram came and there was no reply to his continued and impatient ringing of the bell connected with the next stop, he decided to walk to the great staircase which ascended through the middle of the building. As he walked on, and encountered no one, it became plain that everyone was taking a holiday on this lovely afternoon.

Suddenly, as he turned a corner, he came full upon an open door and found himself staring into a large and lofty room, remarkable for a brilliant red and yellow carpet and ample curtains of grey velvet, which draped high windows opening upon a terrace.

A figure stood upon the terrace, leaning upon the balustrade, and with a disagreeable shock Barry recognized the Colonel.

He stood in the doorway, staring, and dreading to move on lest his movement should be heard.

The Colonel was speaking.

"There it lies . . ." he said in a low, dreamy and per-suasive tone, evidently addressed to someone whom Barry could not see, "my vineyard." He flung out his arms in a yearning gesture towards the coppice. "It is such a small thing to want. Such a little place!"

A murmur, apparently of advice or reproof, sounded across the terrace; and the Colonel impatiently turned away from the balustrade.

"Rights? What rights have they?" he cried.

He leant once more on the balustrade, with his back to Barry, who took the opportunity to hurry on.

He was relieved at his escape from detection, and gave

full attention to reaching the great staircase and proceeding down it and across the hall (deserted save for two sentries, who saluted him) before he allowed his mind to play upon what he had just overheard.

He had no notion of what it meant, but he stowed it away carefully. It might come in useful.

CHAPTER VIII

THE waiter's graves were decently veiled off from the Pleasure Gardens by some old may trees growing along a bank, and wreathed in Traveller's Joy. This was now in flower, and some of the waiters' children were tumbling about on the worn earth under the trees, shaking the blossoms down upon one another while they gnawed shrimps. They were all unusually small and dressed in ragged little vests or chemises that showed their stomachs. Nevertheless, they were laughing as they hopped about. As they were all so small, a shrimp made a mouthful for them and really gave them something to gnaw at.

The Pleasure Gardens were a smallish open space of trampled earth. There was no grass except in the corner nearest the coppice; here the ground was marshy with a small spring which bubbled out of some rocks and spread itself between bright green grass before it ran away into the woods. At one end was a large iron gate set in an iron fence, and beyond this could be seen an ordinary mean London street with a public-house, The Bugle Blast, at one corner. The hum of the city and the smoky smell of it hung over the place.

Beside the stream's source was a cottage. The building had started as a two-roomed dwelling, but the partition dividing the rooms had fallen down and now there was one large room with a window half-veiled by nasturtiums, whose brilliant orange trumpets swung about and looked in. Someone had moved a stone seat into the cottage, and in front of it was a wooden table set with mugs and a tea-urn, a very large loaf and a tin labelled "EDZ."

At one end, on a sheet of newspaper, was a pile of shrimps that smelt of the sea. At the other was an equally large mound of dark green cresses breathing faintly and freshly of the streams from which they came.

The inside walls of the cottage were encrusted with patches of moss and the floor was of stone, but a little woollen mat had been placed immediately below the table to take the chill off anybody's feet. Over the door was written: "H. Sawyer, licensed to sell tea, potatoes, chestnuts, cresses and shrimps," and before the table sat Mrs. Sawyer herself.

She was small and fat and rather like an ageing shrimp, having very small dark eyes in a very red face and a bonnet with two feathers in it that suggested those things shrimps have on their heads. Seated beside her was her daughter, Philly, who was also not unlike a shrimp, but she had very black eyes in a very pink face and that just made the difference. She was plump, and dressed in brown rags, and her hat was a black chip straw, tied round her rough black hair with a spotted red and white handkerchief.

Mr. Sawyer had been a waiter. The Colonel had shot him dead in a temper nearly fifteen years ago when Philly, his only child, was two. Some of the waiters' wives had embroidered "Cu sed Be The Colonel" on a banner made of a bit of old material and presented it solemnly to Mrs. Sawyer on the anniversary of Mr. Sawyer's death, and as she had loved him tenderly and never ceased to grieve for him and miss him, she had felt that she really ought to make use of it. So once a week it was brought out and hung on the wall of the cottage. But one day Philly was boiling the shrimps and wanted a kettle-holder in a hurry, and without thinking she snatched down the banner and used that; and somehow it got to be the kettle-holder.

The Pleasure Gardens had some small flower-beds filled with pansies and love-in-a-mist and mignonette and wall-flowers, while others were planted with radishes and spring onions and lettuces which augmented the waiters' scanty fare. They were small and not very tasty but the waiters found them delicious. A few cresses grew in the stream, too; not large or bold, but better than none. The ones Mrs. Sawyer sold came in every morning from Hatfield in a dashing donkey-cart, and the shrimps came all the way from Southend by the railway. Philly went each day to the station to fetch the basket.

Mrs. Sawyer and Philly slept in the cottage on two long sacks filled with rags. In the summer this was endurable; but they used to be very cold in the dreadful foggy winters, when Mrs. Sawyer sold hot potatoes and chest-nuts, until Lieutenant Toloreaux brought them two beau-tiful thick blankets that he had stolen from the stables. Fancy! they were used to cover the horses!

"He'll be down here this afternoon, mark my words. That's seventy-eight pound you owe me, dear," said Mrs. Sawyer, addressing the first part of her remark to her daughter and the second part to a waiter who had come in for a scoopful of shrimps, with tea and cresses and bread and butter. "A ha'penny on account. Thank you, dear." She wrote some scribbles carefully down in a little book, and smiled at the waiter as he went out.

"There's a nuisance," said Philly. "Me and the children was going to play Fights."

"You needn't stay here for him. He won't want to see you. Lieutenant Toloreaux says he don't care for the female sect. All he wants is to be powerful and rich, poor young man."

"If he sees me a bit of a way off he'll think I'm prettier nor I am and come after me, like that Dannit did."

"Go along with you, he won't."

"Yes he will, and there was a nuisance."

"Go along with you, you know you liked it. You run along off and play your Fights, I'll give Mr. Magnificent his tea and shrimps."

Philly accordingly went to join the children under the may trees and Mrs. Sawyer, who could not read, settled down to await the expected arrival.

When Barry emerged from among the luxuriant and well-tended trees and thick grass of the coppice, the battered and shabby aspect of the pleasure gardens struck him strongly by contrast. And he was disappointed. He had expected a savage, sinister place imbued with the louring spirit of revolution; with perhaps a gin palace where the maddened waiters sought and temporarily found oblivion. The strolling or lounging waiters, the tiny bowling-green, almost bare of grass, now being carefully watered and rolled by two waiters, the children hopping and Mrs. Sawyer presiding over the shrimps, presented a commonplace picture that filled him with disgust. It was a hot afternoon, too—and by now he was thirsty. Must he order tea and drink it in that sordid cabin?

Apparently he must. There was no other place of refreshment in sight except The Bugle Blast, and he was not prepared to go to the trouble of getting the gates open in order to reach that.

He therefore strolled up to the grotto, wherein Mrs. Sawyer was sitting with her hands folded upon her stomach and looking easily at him, and said haughtily:

"Is there tea to be had here, my good woman?"

"Good afternoon. Yes, there are," replied Mrs. Sawyer, neither getting up nor moving her hands.

"Then get me some," said Barry, a little shaken in his

poise because there was nowhere to sit down. He stood looking proudly about him.

"All right. Here it is. Help yourself," said Mrs. Sawyer, removing one hand to point to the urn, the mugs and the shrimps, and then putting it back again.

But this Barry would not endure. He went even paler than his usual hue, flung up his red curls, and commanded icily:

"I said, get me some."

"All right, I will," said Mrs. Sawyer, getting up readily. "I was only having a bit of a sit-down because me legs ache, I didn't mean it spiteful. Shrimps, will you? and cress and bread and butter, too?"

He nodded, still staring disdainfully about him and wishing there were a seat. He was beginning to feel stiff from the morning's exercise.

"If *your* legs ache, you 'ave a bit of a sit-down 'ere." Mrs. Sawyer indicated the stone seat. "Tell you what, I'll put me apron on it. I'm used to it but it might give you a chill."

Her apron had bits of shrimp sticking to it. Barry acknowledged this service with a nod, but as he stooped his head and entered the cool dimness of the grotto that smelled freshly of cresses and fish, he shook out his fine handkerchief and placed it on the apron before he sat down.

After she had served him, Mrs. Sawyer stiffly bent and brought out from somewhere a little tub, which she placed at the cottage door in the sunlight and sat herself slowly upon it. She refolded her hands, leant back against the door frame and once more easily surveyed the scene.

It was not completely disagreeable in the grotto. The patches of moss on the walls looked cool, and the nasturtium leaves and trumpets cast beautiful distorted shadows on the smoky ceiling. The tiny voice of the stream could be heard. The tea tasted of shrimps, but so did everything, and the cresses at least were fit to grace any gentleman's table. But neatness and industry were conspicuous by their absence, and there was nothing to gratify the thoughtful and progressive eye.

Presently his attention was caught by some figures playing under the may trees. A girl in a short brown dress was tumbling about with some children and laughing loudly. Barry was watching them, and musing that the fairest female charms, when unadorned by modesty and elegant clothes, can only excite disgust, when someone came up to the door of the grotto, saying, "Good afternoon, Mrs. Sawyer." It was Lieutenant Toloreaux.

CHAPTER IX

"'ULLO, dear," said Mrs. Sawyer. "''Ave some tea?"

"Thank you." And giving Mrs. Sawyer a pleasant smile, which included Barry, he procured himself some shrimps and tea and sat down on the bench, leaning forward with his cup between his knees and gazing at the players under the may trees.

For some moments they sipped in silence. Then Barry, wondering what was the correct procedure in these circumstances and deciding that it was as well to cultivate everybody unless, of course, they were vulgar or poor, observed:

"You are feeling no stiffness, I trust, from this morning's exercises, Lieutenant Toloreaux?"

"Lord, no," answered Lieutenant Toloreaux, turning to him with a frank and friendly smile. "I took no part in them."

"No part in them?"

"None."

"But you joined in our manœuvres! I myself saw you——"

"Oh, ay, I was there. But I sat still. I contributed neither mind nor muscle to the proceedings."

Barry was so extremely shocked that he was silent. At last he said gravely:

"How can you hope to succeed in a military career if that is your frame of mind?"

"Lord, I don't know!" said the young man heartily. "But consider, when I fail, there will be more room for others."

Barry's first mistrust of Lieutenant Toloreaux was now replaced by the more amiable sentiment of contempt, and he said in a friendlier tone:

"No doubt you are right. By the way, I wish you would enlighten me on one or two points about which I am puzzled."

His companion was silent, but suddenly put a whole lot of shrimps and bread and butter into his mouth.

"It is about the Colonel," pursued Barry, lowering his voice.

"You needn't whisper, dear," said Mrs. Sawyer, turning from her contemplation of the scene, "I know all about everythink. It ain't that I *minds* you whisperin', but it's more conwenient for you not to 'ave to."

"Oh—ah—yes," replied Barry, confused. A little waiter now coming up and requiring Mrs. Sawyer's attention, he went on in the same low tone:

"Yes. About the Colonel. He is a strange man, is he not? Or do you not think so?"

"If you mean why was he sitting in front of all those knives last night, he was doing it to show that he does not fear lightning," said Lieutenant Toloreaux.

"Indeed! Does he often do it?"

"Every so often as there is a storm."

Barry was silent for a moment. Then he went on:

"I take it that the Mess does not approve?"

Lieutenant Toloreaux shook his head and put a lot more bread and butter into it.

"And this afternoon," pursued Barry, suddenly taking a decision and further lowering his voice, "I happened to see something very strange."

Lieutenant Toloreaux nodded.

"I happened to pass an open door and I saw the Colonel stretch out his arms in the direction of that wood." Barry nodded his head towards the coppice, and went on to relate exactly what he had overheard.

His companion continued to eat, but nodded his head comprehendingly at intervals. When Barry had done, he observed:

"It is not strange at all. He wants these Pleasure Gardens."

"But why should he want them?" Barry glanced contemptuously about him. "There is nothing here to gratify a wealthy and fastidious man."

"No, indeed."

"Then why does he want it?"

"Because it does not belong to him."

Barry could understand this and expressed as much in a nod. And then Lieutenant Toloreaux startled him by exclaiming loudly:

"Mrs. Sawyer! He's at it again."

CHAPTER X

"THERE!" said Mrs. Sawyer, turning round from the midst of a small crowd of pale and shabby waiters and one or two soldiers to whom she was dispensing tea: "Didn't you say so!"

Lieutenant Toloreaux nodded. The waiters all turned as one man towards him, looking apprehensive and alarmed: the soldiers looked wooden or wary.

"Wot, again?" said one.

"On'y larst month 'e 'ad a bit 'orf the croquet lawn up the pawk."

"And the munf before that 'e 'ad that 'orse-pond in the wild bit up the Gates," put in an extra large waiter named Thwart.

"'E's got the wood, 'asn't 'e?"

"And four tharsand acres orf the Pawk."

"He taka a bit of da lake-a," put in a dark waiter with an Italian cast of countenance.

"Why carn't 'e be content wif wot 'es got?"

"That's what we'd all like to know," said Mrs. Sawyer.

"But this 'ere is the first time 'e's wanted anythink orf of us," ended Thwart, in a very quiet voice.

Everyone was at once silent, and the hush lasted for some time, as if everyone were thinking over what had just been said. At last the waiter named Sobber, the same who had spoken up when the waiters were summoned to the hall on the day of Barry's arrival, said heavily:

"Well, I reckon it's the Monkey's Allowance again, mates."

There was a disconsolate murmur of agreement, but it was interrupted by the voice of Mrs. Sawyer saying comfortably:

"Get along with you, you've got yer Charter, 'aven't yer?"

Immediately a score of relieved voices exclaimed:

"Cripes, so we 'ave!"

"Blow me over Egypt, I'd forgotten it!"

"That's saved your guns, mates," put in a soldier.

"Good old Charter!"

"Like to see 'im touch our pleasure gardens!"

"Just show 'im the Charter, that'll learn 'im!"

Barry turned to Lieutenant Toloreaux and inquired curiously:

"What is the Charter?"

"Oh lord, I hardly know! It was given to them, so they say, by that old cove General Ramm, don't you know, bestowing the Pleasure Gardens on the waiters for ever."

"And do you think that the Charter will prevent the Colonel from obtaining possession of the pleasure gardens?" Barry went on.

"Cannot shay at all," answered Lieutenant Toloreaux with his mouth full and shaking his head.

"But what is your private opinion?"

"I have none, my dear sir," retorted the Lieutenant cheerfully, rising and going over to the table for a third cup of tea. "Deeds, not words, is my motto."

"But will it not lead to a bloody and exhausting conflict?"

"How can it? What could the waiters do? They are owned by the Colonel; they are slaves. And they have no weapons, except a cannon which that fellow Thwart made in his spare time."

"But if that were placed in one of the towers!" exclaimed Barry, in tones of alarm. "It could command the entrance to the Club——"

"But first it must be got out of the bottle which contains it," interrupted Lieutenant Toloreaux, slapping him on the back and bursting into loud and ill-timed laughter.

"You do not take the situation seriously," said Barry, drawing back and turning pale with temper. "I had supposed these creatures to be your friends."

"No, no; your philoprogenitive faculty has deceived you. Will you take another cup?"

"No, I thank you."

"Then that's ninepence you owe me, dear," called Mrs. Sawyer, from amidst the crowd of waiters which had increased in size and was eagerly discussing the situation.

Barry got up to cross over and pay his account but suddenly realized with dismay that he had not a penny in his pockets. His dinner last night and luncheon this morning had, of course, not been paid for in cash and he had forgotten his lack of money until this moment.

"Broke?" inquired Lieutenant Toloreaux.

After a struggle with himself Barry nodded.

"Never mind, Mrs. Sawyer will trust you."

"Ninepence, dear. Don't forget. Lieutenant Toloreaux'll bring it down some time, won't you, dear? *You* won't be down here again, dear, so I'll say good afternoon."

Barry stiffly inclined his head and the two young men walked away together.

Shadows were falling over the pleasure gardens. The children had gathered round Philly under the trees and she was telling them a story.

When they had left the pleasure gardens and were at the edge of the coppice, Barry said:

"The old hag is right; I shall not come here again."

"I had thought you would not."

"The spectacle of slavery is always disgusting. When the slaves have not the spirit to rebel it becomes trebly so."

Lieutenant Toloreaux shook his head and sighed.

"I despair of mankind," pursued Barry.

Lieutenant Toloreaux jumped sideways over a stone and observed:

"No doubt you are right."

"The Colonel is justified in taking anything away from wretches sunk so low that they will not defend it."

"Come, come, it has not come to that yet. I have some hopes that Pillichoddie may persuade the Colonel not to take action."

"Has Pillichoddie much influence with the Colonel?"

"So it is said. And, indeed, it appears so."

"I hope that he will not dissuade him!" cried Barry ardently, pausing at the edge of the wood with the sunset upon his face. "I love a struggle! I would wish to see the waiters crushed—the pleasure gardens wrested from them, the Colonel triumphant."

"It is highly likely that you will get your wish," said Lieutenant Toloreaux.

"I am on the Colonel's side," continued Barry, but in cooler tones; he was already wondering if he should have betrayed his sentiments so plainly. "I foresee there must be a vast amount of diplomacy in this matter; comings and goings, consultations, conferences, delicate adjustments, and I shall—but what is the matter? I fear you are ill?"

Lieutenant Toloreaux, who had been groaning loudly throughout the latter part of Barry's speech, shook his head. "No. But I want some more shrimps. I will, with your permission, bid you good evening."

"Good evening," answered Barry, his legs somewhat knocked from under him by this rapid departure. He would have liked to go on talking about the situation; but instead he walked home alone, musing upon it and deciding that there would be plenty of opportunities for a clever and cautious young man to benefit from what would occur.

· · · · ·

Lieutenant Toloreaux retraced his steps towards the Pleasure Gardens. Philly, who had watched his departure from under the may tree as she sat with the children, now came running towards him and threw her arms about his neck.

"Dearest love!" he exclaimed when they had fondly kissed.

"Oh, I *am* so glad you have come back! I was afraid you might be going off without speaking to me."

"Now, Philly! How can you be so foolish when you know how dearly I love you?"

She hung her head and blushed. "You say you do, Lieutenant Toloreaux——"

"Gerard."

"Gerard, then—and I believe you, of course, but——"

"But what, my darling girl?"

"It's the Fishes," she whispered, so quietly that he could hardly hear. "I do try to wash myself clean but I know I smell of them."

Lieutenant Toloreaux stood back from her a little, with his arms still about her, and studied her rosy face and troubled grey eyes with a considering air.

"Yes," he said at last, "you do. But I don't mind. It reminds me of being by the sea in Devon, when I was a young one and as happy as the day was long. I like it," and once more he kissed her.

They began to stroll back towards the may trees, entwined.

"As happy as the day was long!" repeated Philly. "I expect you often wish them days was back again."

"Indeed I don't," he returned stoutly. "For in those days I hadn't got you, my dearest girl. And, besides, when we are married I shall go there again, and live beside the sea with you in a little white house——"

"With sunflowers in the garden——"

"And a cuckoo clock in the nursery——"

"And a kitten——"

"And toast for tea every day——"

"Oh, we shall be so happy!"

"Oh, we shall be so happy!" they cried together, stopping in their walk and exchanging another tender kiss.

Mrs. Sawyer, benignly observing from afar, now waved to them, but they did not see.

"I don't suppose," said Philly rather timidly, when they

were seated upon some worn old roots under the trees,
"that you have heard from them gentlemen again?"

"The solicitors? No, my love."

"And the last they said was——"

"That I should hear from them on the thirty-first of
October."

"The thirty-first of October," murmured Philly. "Oh,
I do wonder how much it will be."

"Two thousand pounds, I have always heard."

"Is there so much money in the world!" sighed Philly.

The fact that they indulged themselves in this conversation almost every time they met in no way detracted from
its magic but rather added to it, as repetition increases
the power of a spell.

"A thousand pounds to buy you out of the Army——"
went on Philly.

"—and the other thousand to buy the little white house,
the sunflowers, the cuckoo clock, the toast and the
kitten."

"Oh, Lieutenant Toloreaux—Gerard, I mean!"

"Oh, Philly!"

While the flowers of Travellers' Joy fell slowly through
the evening light, they kissed again and again.

CHAPTER XI

A WEEK passed agreeably. Barry attended reviews
and drills or studied military text-books by day, and
at night accompanied Captain Gabriel and Lieutenant
Toloreaux (the two were close friends), or the two
Ensigns, Cusset and Dannit, to places of amusement. He
had repaid Captain Gabriel's debt from his first pay, which

was generous; and nothing more about money had passed between Lieutenant Toloreaux and himself save the repayment of the ninepence.

Captain Gabriel's aunt, Lady Venner, had a large town house where she gave handsome, if not brilliant, balls, and several times the young officers encountered Miss Pressure at these receptions. But she was always accompanied by Doctor Pressure, who was apt to come over all of a doo-da in the heat of a crowded ballroom and have to go and sit in a little den full of palms and sip soda-water while his daughter fanned him. Barry derived entertainment from observing how the Doctor's attacks always coincided with a request from Captain Gabriel that Miss Beatrice should dance with him, but Cussett and Dannit said hotly that it was a hanged shame and that the old skinamaree deserved to burn.

Barry heard no open discussion of the Colonel's wish to add the Pleasure Gardens to the Regiment's estates, but he gathered from scraps of gossip, hints and an increasing atmosphere of tension and excitement that the other officers were fully aware of the situation: and that while Major Baird, Captain Gabriel and Cussett and Dannit supported the Colonel's ambitions, in some cases from a desire to please him and in some from the wish to increase the power and possessions of the Regiment, Lieutenant Toloreaux, Major Milde and Major Pillichoddie were in the opposite camp.

Major Pillichoddie, eldest of the officers, had served for many years under the venerable General Ramm, founder of the Regiment, the Club and the Military School. He it was who had supported the expiring General upon the battlefield and received from him, during the day and night before they were rescued, a number of household hints, including an awfully good hair tonic that the Major had graciously made public. It was called "Whisker-ando," and the sale of it at 1s. 6d. a bottle added a com-

fortable annual sum to the Regiment's funds. Major
Pillichoddie was naturally held in some veneration by
his brother officers and especially by the Colonel, and the
fact that he drank heavily (because he liked it, not because
he was miserable) had not modified their attitude towards
him. When it did show signs of waning, the Major produced from the ancient Hindoo chests in which he kept
them another of General Ramm's recipes, and the awe
was re-established.

Major Pillichoddie also stood high in favour with the
Queen, who welcomed any hints that might assist her in
reducing the very large yearly expenditure at the Club,
and she was particularly interested in General Ramm's
collection because it was reputed to have been imparted
to him verbally by a Hindoo, one of her faithful Indian
subjects, in gratitude for a favour General Ramm had
once done him. There was a section of the private soldiers
that flatly refused to believe General Ramm could ever
have done any Hindoo a favour, except the negative one
of keeping out of his way; be that as it may, it was the
habit of Major Pillichoddie to repair to the Palace once
a month, just before Her Majesty inspected the Club's
account books, and impart to her a domestic economy
hint—some tip for more persuasively rendering mutton
fat, a whisper about preserving the water in which rice
had been boiled in order to starch handkerchiefs, a reve-
lation that potato peelings will effectively clean soiled gilt
picture frames—to put her into a better humour when she
arrived to make the rounds. This custom was approved by
the Colonel.

Cussett and Dannit came frequently into contact with
Major Pillichoddie in the course of their duties, and chafed
at the severity of his commands. They were ever on the
lookout to see in what way they could injure him and
lessen his influence with the Colonel, and were doubly
anxious that the Colonel should secure the pleasure

gardens, because Major Pillichoddie was opposed to his doing so.

One evening, when they were about to set out with Barry for a conversazione (with music and ices) at Lady Venner's, Dannit said:

"I will tell you what, my dear fellows, do not let us go! We will go to The Bugle Blast instead, and I will show you something that will surprise you."

"The Bugle Blast?" said Barry doubtfully. "Is not that a public-house?"

"Indeed it is, with a fine barmaid," cried Cussett.

"But will not the company be low? Surely we shall meet no one of importance there?"

"Who knows? We will try our luck. And the beer is good, and if Bella is in the humour she will sing 'The Ballad of Fly Bessie' to us."

Barry was not attracted by the picture presented, and he also feared to offend Lady Venner by not going to her conversazione, but he allowed himself to be persuaded because he suspected that Dannit had some good reason for suggesting the plan.

Half an hour later, having found their way through the squalid and ill-lit streets where lived the waiters' wives and children, the three young gentlemen stepped into the saloon bar of The Bugle Blast.

A crowd of bagmen, bargees from the nearby Regent's Park Canal, and soldiers in their beautiful scarlet coats and caps pushed back on their heads, was lounging at the bar roaring the chorus of a song:

> But Bessie was sly,
> Bessie was fly,
> She said, "Do you see any green in my eye?"

and waving their tankards and cigars in the bright, smoky air. There was a strong smell of beer and gin.

Barry's attention was caught by what he at first supposed to be a large jar of barley sugars, just visible between the crowding heads of the customers; but as one of them moved aside he perceived that the objects were in fact yellow curls. They adorned the head of a plump woman in a plaid dress of red, dark green and maroon.

Cussett and Dannit thrust their way into the crowd, crying "Hulloa, Bella!" and Barry followed more slowly.

"Good evenin', young gents," cried Bella, waving a red hand adorned with jet rings. "Haven't seen you this ten days. Come in for a sting-and-fizzer, have you? Very refreshin' on a hot night, eh, gentlemen?"

The crowd shouted agreement, and watched with interest while Barry was presented to Bella; she, despite his first dislike of her coarse appearance and loud dress, won back a measure of his approval by the respectful manner in which she said "Good evenin', sir. Honoured to see you here."

Even this creature recognizes a gentleman, he thought, as he retired with Cussett and Dannit to a table where the sting-and-fizzers were presently brought to them by a potboy.

His companions were of that enormous and healthy human company that relishes sitting for hours in a crowded and overheated room, steadily distending the stomach with liquid while breathing tobacco smoke and roaring songs until the eyes are smarting and the throat raw. There must be pleasure in these actions; it is impossible that countless generations should have enjoyed doing them without there being some delights concealed therein. Nevertheless, after conducting an examination into these practices extending over some twenty years, an examination theoretical and practical, impartial and exhaustive, sympathetic and scientific, there *are* persons who can only explain the popularity of such evenings on the assumption that three-quarters of the human race delights in martyrdom.

Barry soon found his surroundings excessively tedious and began to regret heartily that they had not gone to Lady Venner's reception.

It was while he was musing thus, with eyes fixed idly upon the doors of the apartment, that these doors opened and a slight figure stood there, shrinkingly surveying the scene. It was a boy of some fifteen years, shabbily but neatly dressed in black.

After observing the various groups gathered by the bar with their glasses, the boy straightened his shoulders, sighed deeply, and advanced into the room.

One of the rough fellows round Bella happened to turn at this instant, and caught sight of him. At once he roared—

"Drink up, boys, quick! 'Ere comes young Licker!"

CHAPTER XII

HIS companions at once drained their glasses, clapped them down, and glared defiantly at the boy, who had come to a stop before the bar and was now facing them with a reproachful look.

"Men, men!" he cried in a low ringing voice. "What do I see here?—Drink, waste, debauchery, ignorance, RUIN!"

"Go hon!"

"Pshaw!"

"Fiddledeedee!"

"Where's the harm in a glass, I'd like to know?"

"Plenty of harm. Disgrace and ruin," repeated George Licker, his blue eye roving sadly yet keenly among the glasses upon the bar. "Men, though most of you are old

enough to be my dads, I can't abear to see you a-taking
of the wrong path. Won't you cast the deadly potion
aside?"

"No!" roared everybody.

"Before it is too late!" implored George Licker.

A little man who had been furtively trying to finish
his pint without George observing him here had the
misfortune to drop his clay pipe, and at once George
turned upon him.

"Sobber!" he cried ringingly, advancing upon the little
man. "Give up your tipple! Give it up, I say!"

"If your Pa was 'ere, young George, he wouldn't 'arf
paste you," said Sobber, sheltering his beer behind his
hand and retreating as far as possible towards the bar.
"I'm blowed if I gives it up!"

"My Pa approves of my life work, Arthur Sobber. Do
not strive to create dissension between parent and child.
Instead, set down that vile brew and vow to swill no
more!"

"Shan't!" retorted Arthur Sobber, passionately. "I'll
drink it up this minute, I will, so there, see?"

"You shall not!" cried George, darting forward and
snatching the mug from his hand. "Sooner will I drink
it myself!"

So saying, he lifted the mug to his lips and unhesitatingly
drained the contents to the dregs.

A roar of mingled derision and anger now burst from
the crowd, and several of the men made their way to
George and ran him out of the bar; but not before he had,
quick as lightning, drained several more cans. The doors
slammed upon him as he was thrown into the darkness,
shouting:

"Cast it down! Cast it down! Vow to swill no more!"

A pause followed, in which everyone refreshed themselves after their exertions.

"The next item on the programme will be Father

Doogood, mates," said a soldier gloomily. "Waiting outside as usual, I reckon."

"Hold your fire!"

"Now, now," reproved Bella, flicking at the potboy with a glass cloth. "I'm sure Father Doogood's a very nice gentleman and does a lot of good."

"I never said 'e wasn't. But yer don't want to be done good in a pub, do yer, cullies?"

A roar of assent, in the midst of which the doors opened again and two figures entered.

The first was a priest with a hopeful face, the second a large, elderly stiff figure in a gorgeous purple overcoat that gleamed with copper braid like a Burmese idol, whom Barry recognized as Major Pillichoddie.

"Egad!" cried Cussett, staring. "Do my eyes deceive me?"

"I had vowed to give you a surprise," replied Dannit in a gratified tone. "Confess, are you not amazed?"

"Flabbergasted, indeed. I had no idea this was one of his haunts."

"Yet it is, and has been this many a week."

The crowd had doffed its hats with rough respect at the entry of the soldier and the priest, but replaced them again as Major Pillichoddie, followed by the breathlessly attentive gaze of Barry and the two ensigns (whom he had not observed) disappeared into a little room curtained off from the bar by some red plush. Slowly their mouths opened, and their chins dropped as he was followed the next moment by Bella. The red curtain fell to behind them.

"Crack my trunnions!" breathed Cussett at last.

Dannit nodded triumphantly.

"How delighted the Colonel would be!" pursued Cussett. "His favourite, the intimate of General Ramm, the conveyor of recipes to the Queen, dallying with a barmaid!"

"Yet I have not the slightest doubt that their dalliance is innocent," drawled Dannit, without mockery.

"Nor I," answered Cussett at once.

"Come, now——!" Barry rallied them.

"You do not know Major Pillichoddie." Both his comrades turned upon him eagerly. "He takes no interest in the fair sex. He cares only for the Regiment."

Barry was about to dispute this, when he became aware of a hand in a black woollen glove thrusting a sheet of paper under his nose. Affronted, he drew back, but could not help reading:

EVIL COMMUNICATIONS CORRUPT GOOD MANNERS.

It was Father Doogood, who gave him a reproving smile and shake of the head as he glided away to distribute other papers among the bar-flies, inscribed: "It is better to be good than to be bad," "Do not swear," "Do not drink," "Do not bash people in the face," "Do not steal," "Do not break Commandment No. 7."

"What impertinence!" Barry was pale with rage as he screwed up the paper.

Father Doogood was now, amid a hush of amazement and horror, drawing aside the red plush curtain preparatory to delivering a paper on which was written—as everyone took care to see—

IT IS BETTER TO MARRY THAN TO BURN.

"Merciful Heavens!" muttered Cussett, half rising in his chair.

But as the curtain was drawn aside and the scene within was revealed, the spectators breathed again. Major Pillichoddie sat upright before the fire sipping a brandy, and Bella sat by him, but at a respectful distance, sewing at a loose cockade upon his hat. Father Doogood placed the paper upon the Major's knee; the Major picked it up, read it, ejaculated:

"Ha! Very proper, very right," and twisted it into a spill with which he lit a cigar for himself, at the same time offering his case to Father Doogood, who accepted one and seated himself by the fire. The curtain fell upon them; and the crowd broke into a new buzz of conversation. In a few moments Bella returned to her place behind the bar.

"Dannit!" Cussett leaned across and eagerly addressed his friend. "Molloy—you too! I have a magnificent idea—an idea that will cook Pillichoddie's goose with the Colonel, and gain the latter the pleasure gardens. Listen to me!"

CHAPTER XIII

ON a sunny morning a week or so later Beatrice might have been observed with her maid, Sour, entering the portals of the South Kensington Museum.

The maid carried some note-books, a folding stool, a large black umbrella and a tract entitled, *The Mad Machine-Minder's Daughter*; the mistress was laden only with a white reticule containing some smelling-salts, a lace handkerchief and the stump of a cigar.

"I expect to be some time, Sour," observed Beatrice as they entered the Untipped Flint Arrow Heads, Stone Spears and Javelins Room. "Doctor Pressure requires drawings, with notes, of every type of arrow, spear and javelin."

"Very good, miss."

"You need not follow me from case to case." She glanced down their well-polished ranks and suppressed a sigh. "You can sit by the javelins."

"Very good, miss. How if they explode, miss?"

"There is no need for alarm, I assure you, Sour. They are not guns."

"It's all the same, miss. If I lose sight of you behind the cases, miss, I'll holler."

"I hardly think——"

"Oh yes, miss, I'll holler at once." She lowered her voice and glanced round. "There's Men about, miss. I saw one a-lurking be'ind the door."

"It was only the attendant, Sour."

"It's all the same, miss, and a young lady can't be too careful."

She unfolded the stool, seated herself upon it and laid the umbrella on the floor, unfolded *The Mad Machine-Minder's Daughter*, and began to read, muttering the words over to herself as she did so.

Beatrice took up her position in front of the first case, opened a note-book and began to draw.

It was quiet in the museum. Long rays of sunlight poured through the lofty windows. Outside, a green tree waved silently to and fro against the blue sky and the motionless white clouds, already tender with autumn.

Beatrice worked on; only once raising her eyes from the delicate sketch she was making to gaze for a moment at the sunlight; then resolutely turning again to her task.

An hour passed thus. She had finished with the first case and was standing by the second making notes on a notched and corrugated stabbing spear, when a voice asked cheerfully:

"My dear, have you such a thing as a pin?"

Startled, she looked up.

A lady stood there, smiling, dressed in dove-grey cashmere and black lace with some late roses at her bosom; her brown eyes sparkled under a bonnet trimmed with a wonderful bird of paradise in every shade of red and green. In one gloved hand she was holding a strip of lace that vanished beneath the hem of her walking dress; it was torn.

Beatrice was a little shocked at the cheerfulness and ease of the lady's manner, and also at her request; she was rather dazzled, too, by the extreme beauty of her figure (which even she could tell was perfect) and by her startling yet pleasing style of dress.

She answered politely:

"I am sorry; I have none. Perhaps my maid——"

"Oh, pray let us not disturb her," said the lady quickly. "I will tear it off," and before Beatrice could stop her she had ripped the shred of lace apart in her teeth. "There!" she said, kicking the hem of her dress slightly to and fro, "does it show?"

Beatrice surveyed the braided hem and small foot in a bronze kid boot and shook her head. She felt almost irresistibly drawn to this lady, whose chestnut curls and pale brown complexion were so unusual, but she was certainly not like any other lady she had ever met before, and she had a strong feeling that Doctor Pressure and Sour and all her acquaintances would not have approved of her at all.

"Capital!" cried the lady. "Now I can walk to my carriage in comfort. I am sorry I disturbed you, my dear. What are you drawing so busily?"

Beatrice, secretly relieved to have an excuse for resting a moment, held out her note-book.

"A dear little spear!" cried the lady, peering. "Is it to please yourself, my dear? Are you interested in little spears?"

"Oh, no. I am making notes for my papa."

"And your papa is?"

"Doctor Harrovius Pressure, Headmaster of the First Bloods' Military Preparatory School."

"Indeed? He must be very clever."

"He is," replied Beatrice.

"And you——" pursued the lady, drawing closer so that a breath of perfume from the roses floated over Beatrice, "are you yourself clever?"

"I fear not, but naturally my papa's interests are mine."

"Indeed? On such a lovely morning, when most girls are riding in the park or shopping with their mammas?"

"I cannot ride and I have no mamma. She is in Heaven."

"Is she really, though!" said the lady, nodding the bird of paradise so that the reflection of its red tail plumes danced in the polished floor. "How sad for you and your papa."

Beatrice was silent, thinking of the portrait of a large and severe lady in mouse velvet without much hair that hung in Doctor Pressure's study.

"No doubt," the lady went on, "you and he are very devoted?"

Beatrice hesitated. Truth struggled with loyalty.

"He is so clever——" she said faintly at last. "He has not time, naturally, to——"

"To spare for the company of his daughter. Are you an only child, my dear?"

Beatrice nodded.

"And you are not betrothed?"

This time Beatrice shook her head. Her perfect honesty forbade her to turn away or lower her gaze and a deep blush came up into her face. Her distress was augmented by her sudden realization that she *had* a pin in her reticule but had automatically denied the fact in order to avoid any danger of exposing the cigar stump.

"You surprise me. You are very handsome."

"Handsome? I?"

"Certainly. You are a little too pale, it is true, and— who makes your boots, my dear?"

"Tender and True, of Jermyn Street." Beatrice felt

dazed and answered mechanically; she was trying, much against her will, to summon her self-possession to rebuke the lady.

"They do not quite fit about the ankle. Now my own people, Heel and Toe, of Bedford Street——"

"Pray, forgive me," Beatrice falteringly interrupted her, "but I do not think that you should say I am—am—handsome."

"And why is that?" The lady suddenly slipped an arm about her waist and gave her a little shake, with such a smile that it was not easy to go on. "Don't you think it's true?"

"No—but—it encourages worldly thoughts——" stammered Beatrice, "and all our hopes, surely, should be set on Heaven."

"True. And your gloves, my dear? Marshall and Snelgrove?"

"Debenham and Freebody. For our life here is only a preparation for a better one."

"No doubt. Do you choose your bonnets yourself?"

Beatrice explained that she was a lady-in-waiting and therefore had to dress chiefly as the Queen's taste dictated.

The lady listened, her arm still about the girl's waist, and although Beatrice was uneasy about it all—her dress, her frivolous manner, her curiosity—she also experienced an unfamiliar happiness in being thus questioned about her clothes. Doctor Pressure did not even know that such things existed, any more than an untamed buffalo of the jungles would have; he signed the cheques for her modest bills and, so to speak, galloped snorting away.

At this point their conversation was interrupted by a distant mooing.

"S'sh!" The lady held up one finger. "Somebody hol—was that somebody calling?"

"It is my maid. She has evidently become alarmed by my absence." And Beatrice, gently disengaging herself from her companion's arm, stepped out beyond the cases and showed herself to Sour, who was peering sharply behind each one as if to pounce upon a lurking man. The lady, arranging her roses, slowly followed.

"It is nearly one o'clock, miss, and the carriage was to be there at one sharp," said Sour, approaching with a suspicious eye fixed on the lady.

"I know, Sour; I am coming now."

"I quite wondered what had become of you, miss. I thought some man had crept up behind you stealthy-like and suddenly flung his arm round your neck with one hand, miss, while he stabbed you with one of those knife-things they always carry with the other, miss."

"No, Sour. It was kind of you to be alarmed, but I am, as you see, quite safe."

"Yes, miss, so far."

Beatrice now turned to bow to the lady in farewell, but the latter took her hand and held it.

"You will come and see me, will you not?" she said, smiling. A dimple appeared in one pale brown cheek and Beatrice could not take her eyes from it.

"It is most kind of you," she said with embarrassment, "but——"

"The Doctor doesn't like you to go visiting, Miss, you know, especially to persons we don't know who they may be," put in Sour, her beady eyes running over the orange silk that lined the lady's bonnet, the paradise bird, the long curve of her waist, her bronze boots.

"My name is Mrs. Lovecome," the lady went on, looking in her reticule, "and my address is 24——"

"Acacia Road, St. John's Wood," muttered Sour.

"——Belgrave Square," went on Mrs. Lovecome calmly, handing Beatrice a card. "I am at home on Thursdays, but pray come on any day at four. I think we have a mutual acquaintance in Lady Venner."

"Yes, indeed, I sometimes go to her conversaziones," said Beatrice, smiling and more at ease.

"Indeed? I shall hope to see you at her ball on Saturday; I am to sing."

"Oh, do you sing? How—how delightful."

"I am a singer," corrected Mrs. Lovecome, while Sour silently drew out a large green bottle of smelling-salts and leant against the neolithic flints with her eyes shut.

Beatrice looked politely puzzled.

"I earn my living by singing," explained Mrs. Lovecome. "And I am also *directrice*—'headmistress' is the new word, is it not?—of a school for young ladies."

Between bewilderment, apprehension and fascination, Beatrice could only smile and return the pressure of the hand that held her own and murmur that she would do her best to come, if her papa's permission could be obtained.

Mrs. Lovecome then strode—she had such a free and graceful walk that the word came irresistibly to mind as one watched her—away, and Beatrice and Sour made their way to the carriage.

"I'm sure your dear papa would never let you go a-calling on a person of that sort, Miss," said Sour on the way home. "A singer! and a sort of governess! Never heard of such a thing in all my natural. Earning her own living, indeed!" Sour tossed a very large rusty black bonnet like an old mussel shell, with grey bead trimmings like winkles. "A very strange sort of person indeed *I* thought her, Miss."

But Beatrice was silent. Another face had come to smile beside the one that was always in her heart.

CHAPTER XIV

THE evening of Saturday was clear and fine. About half-past ten, just as the carriages were rolling up to the door of Lady Venner's house bringing guests to the ball, three figures might have been observed pacing slowly, arm-in-arm, up and down outside The Bugle Blast. They were Cussett and Dannit, with their arms firmly linked in those of Father Doogood, who kept glancing longingly towards the public-house.

"—Surely you believe it's right to marry people?" Cussset was saying.

"Sure I do, but only if they're after wishing it."

"They do wish it. They are quite devoted to one another. You must have seen that. He goes there every night."

"'Tis under the influence of strong drink, he is."

"Nonsense, man! Sober as a judge. No, 'tis the tender passion takes him there."

"And think of their souls!" put in Dannit.

"I wish you would be letting me away to me duties. I have all these"—Father Doogood shook some leaflets he carried—"to deliver in there before midnight."

"Living in sin!" said Cussett.

"'Tis a dreadful thing, no doubt." Father Doogood shook his head and sighed.

"Then put it right!" The young men spoke in chorus, shaking his arms vigorously. "All you have to do is to go in there when they're together, and marry them. Two souls saved!"

"Mrs. Bella would never consent."

"I'll lay she will!" cried Cussett. "A gentleman for a husband, in a fine uniform! Of course she will consent. Come, we will ask her now!" and he started towards The Bugle Blast, flinging back his handsome head to throw

a wild wink at Dannit as he dragged his companions with
him.

. . . . .

Major Pillichoddie was being dressed by his batman for
Lady Venner's ball.

Tall, stiff, silent, he stood in front of the glass while the
servant buckled the straps under his shoes. His square red
face was expressionless, his mighty shoulders were held as
straight as ever they had been during his forty years in the
Regiment.

His rooms lacked the luxurious appointments of those
of the other officers. A large white thin bed that sagged
in the middle, two swords crossed above the mantelpiece,
some well-worn volumes on Strategy and Tactics, and two
daguerreotypes completed the furnishings. One was of
General Ramm; the other of a terrier dog that the Major
had once owned.

The servant finished his task and stood up.

"All correct, sir."

"Ah—thank you, Pound. I shall be late. You may
go to bed. 'Night to you."

"Good night, sir."

With his busby under one arm and his coat swinging
from his shoulders, Major Pillichoddie walked swayingly
out. Pound put away the whisky, after pouring himself a
tot, and sat down to read the paper.

. . . . .

Most of the Regiment was at Lady Venner's that evening, and Doctor Pressure had been persuaded to leave his
study and grace the proceedings. He was all done up in
an evening suit, distinguishedly baggy at the knees, and
some rather phoney foreign Orders, consisting of a lot of
coloured ribbons and some tarnished silver-gilt eagles and
things. These had been bestowed on him by potentates
whose sons had passed through the Military School at

different times. He was standing conveniently near a little
alcove with a chair and some palms in it, just in case
Captain Gabriel asked to dance with Beatrice, and gazing
gloomily at the lighthearted throng. So had the Assyrians
danced (thought Doctor Pressure) and the Babylonians;
likewise the Etruscans, the Ephesians and the Phœnicians.
And what were they now? BONES.

"Cup, sir?" inquired a footman.

Doctor Pressure waved it away.

"Papa?" Beatrice and her partner, Barry, halted
opposite Doctor Pressure as the music ceased. "Are you
feeling quite well, dear papa?" she went on timidly, trying
not to glance at the alcove. "You—you—would not like
me to sit with you a little and fan you?"

"I am perfectly well, I thank you, Beatrice. So far, at
least." He morosely studied her white crinoline and green
wreath, then put out a hand in a large crumpled glove and
dabbed at the side of her head. "You have something—
there is a part of your person that seems to need adjustment—*just here*," and he pulled it.

"Oh, no—thank you, Papa, but that is—is—meant to
be there. It—it is a curl."

"Indeed," said Doctor Pressure, awfully, and his gaze
passed to Barry. "You seem overheated, young man."
Though his manner was crushing, he did not object to
Barry as violently as to most of the officers; he had even
permitted Beatrice to waltz with him, for he divined that
the young man's interests were elsewhere.

"The rooms are warm," replied Barry, not pleased
that his flushed face had been noticed. The evening was
being a dull one; Miss Pressure had not a word to say for
herself, his other partners did not seem to him attractive,
and his boon companions, Cussett and Dannit, were absent.

"Only to those who foolishly gyrate about them."

Barry bowed and was silent, pressing his handkerchief
to his brow.

The dancers were now seating themselves on gilt chairs beneath the palms and azaleas about a piano.

"Madame Jeanne is going to sing," said Beatrice, turning to Barry.

"Charming. Do you like to stay and listen or would you prefer an ice in the conservatory?"

"Beatrice," commanded Doctor Pressure, retreating into the alcove, "the fan!"

He sat down and shut his eyes, and Beatrice, anxiously bending over him, began to fan him with a small lace one from her reticule.

"You will excuse me?" asked Barry, bowing.

She inclined her head, and he retired.

From where she was sitting, Beatrice could see the piano, and in a moment Mrs. Lovecome, professionally known as Madame Jeanne, walked out and stood beside it. She wore a soft red dress that displayed the pale brown beauty of her arms, and had some blue flowers in her chestnut hair.

Barry, who was crossing the room towards the supper-room at the same moment, also saw her, and stopped. A violent pain struck his heart: for a confused second he thought he was stabbed. Then he slowly sat down on the nearest chair, trembling, and never taking his gaze from her face.

Mrs. Lovecome smiled at the accompanist, the first chords were struck, and then she began to sing in a rounded warm contralto:

> "O my Luve's like a red, red rose
> That's newly sprung in June——"

Beatrice, still fanning her father, listened with a growing happiness. The air, the music of the lovely voice, soothed and charmed her as no other sound had ever done, and she watched Mrs. Lovecome's every movement.

"Fiddle-faddle!" said Doctor Pressure violently, sitting

up and opening his eyes and pushing the fan away. "There, there, that will do; when this caterwauling is over you can send one of those whippersnappers to get me some toast and water. Why I came here I do not know. I *do— not—know*."

The song ended; applause was given; and after a pause Signor Bello broke into "O Sole Mio."

Beatrice and her father remained seated in the little alcove, while Doctor Pressure made his daughter polish his spectacles and sew a button on his glove with the housewife she always carried. She had seen Captain Gabriel looking hopelessly about the room a moment since, and her heart swelled with unhappiness and longing, but it was no use; she was a prisoner.

It was while she was trying to adjust one of the foreign decorations, whose pin had come off, that Beatrice heard a light step at the entrance to the alcove. She glanced up, and saw Mrs. Lovecome. At the same instant Doctor Pressure sprang to his feet, gasping:

"Jenny!"

CHAPTER XV

"JANE, that is, I should say. Jane." He corrected himself instantly. "Ah—that is——" His voice died away as he stared at her, opening and shutting his mouth. Beatrice looked from one to the other, bewildered, and another of the phoney orders slipped its moorings and fell to the floor.

"Why, Doctor Pressure!" said Mrs. Lovecome, holding out her hand, which Doctor Pressure did not take. "How very delightful to see you again. Your papa and I used to

know one another, my dear, many years ago," turning
to Beatrice.

"Many years ago," repeated Dr. Pressure, nodding.

"But we had quite lost touch with one another," went
on Mrs. Lovecome.

"Touch with one another," repeated Doctor Pressure,
staring glassily.

"In fact, I sometimes feared he was dead."

"Feared he was dead."

"But now that we have met again, and I find that he
has a charming daughter, we must all see a good deal of
each other, must we not?"

"Must we not."

"I made acquaintance with your daughter in the
museum the other morning, Doctor Pressure. I asked her
for a pin, did I not, my dear?"

"A pin?" For the first time Doctor Pressure turned
upon Beatrice and glared suspiciously at her: what had
she been keeping from him?

"Yes. I had torn my—a piece of lace," said Mrs.
Lovecome, stooping as easily as a girl to pick up the
phoney eagle. "Shall I put this on for you, Doctor
Pressure?"

"No—no, I thank you!" said Doctor Pressure hoarsely,
retreating from her. "Beatrice will adjust it for me."

"Oh, I am sure Beatrice would prefer to dance," said
Mrs. Lovecome. "There is a young man over there who
seems to lack a partner, I will call him in," and, ignoring
the furious glare of Doctor Pressure and the frightened gasp
of Beatrice, she advanced to the door and addressed one of
a group of gentlemen which seemed to have collected there:

"Ah! Lieutenant Toloreaux, will you, in the goodness
of your heart, be my messenger?"

"Oh, by George, yes, Madame Jeanne!"

"Then will you tell Captain Venner that I particularly
wish to speak to him?"

Ticky, looking delighted, darted away to find his friend, and another officer, with red curls, who had been silently watching Mrs Lovecome, now approached Beatrice and said something in a low tone.

"Mrs. Lovecome," said Beatrice in a moment falteringly (for she saw Ticky approaching with Captain Gabriel), "may I present Lieutenant Molloy?"

"I am charmed."

Barry bowed over her hand in its long glove, but could not speak.

Doctor Pressure, meanwhile, had sat down once more upon his little gilt chair, but so heavily, in his agitation, that it gave an ominous creak and he had to get up again. He glanced round in despair. Where was Beatrice—the fan—the toast and water—all his comforts? Gone, fled. He was alone with six whippersnappers and Mrs. Lovecome, and another decoration was working loose. He had two (the Peruvian and the Montenegrin) in his pocket already.

"Madame Jeanne desires——?" said Captain Gabriel, looming enormously over her with his kind, sad smile.

"I have a great honour for you," said Mrs. Lovecome gaily, taking him by the hand. "You know Miss Pressure —do you not?—yes, I thought so—Doctor Pressure does not care for her to dance more than twice in the evening, but he has chosen you for her second partner." And she led him up to Beatrice and put her hand in his.

A kind of cross between a snort and a bellow broke forth from the alcove as the two glided away in the first steps of a waltz, but neither Beatrice nor Gabriel heard; and a wall of officers, in front of which Mrs. Lovecome stood smiling and slowly waving her blue fan, shut off the alcove from the general view. Occasionally a faint tinkle sounded as Doctor Pressure, tramping up and down beneath the palms, shook off another decoration.

Ah, what happiness to be at last alone! To look down

into the beloved eyes that for so many long nights have been bathed in hopeless tears! Gently to guide those little feet in their white satin slippers into the mazes of the dance! How obediently she answers to the lightest touch! Her brown head is smooth and brilliant as satin, crowned with the tiny bitter leaves of ivy. The coral cross rises and falls quickly on her white neck. He can count the dark lashes on her cheek. *Look up at me, Beatrice. Ah, why must this ever end?*

"Now you must all go away——" said Mrs. Lovecome.

"Oh, I say, Madame Jeanne!"

"——because I want to talk to Doctor Pressure. He and I are old acquaintances and we have not met for years. Yes, I mean it. Go, now."

Laughing and protesting, they strolled off; Barry to find his cloak and leave the ball immediately. He was horrified by what had happened to him: every moment passed in her presence deepened the terrible enchantment and he must be alone to think.

"Now, Harrovius," said Mrs. Lovecome kindly, going back into the alcove and picking her way round a Circassion Order of the Royal Antechamber and a Japanese Third Degree of the Umbrella Over the Imperial Teapot, "do make yourself comfortable."

"I shall never be comfortable again," replied Doctor Pressure stonily.

"Oh, yes you will," retorted Mrs. Lovecome cheerfully, picking up some of the ribbon off the decorations and beginning to roll it. "I expect you will be very comfortable in bed to-night. You always used to be."

"Woman," said Doctor Pressure in a terrible voice—rather spoilt by having to be a whisper—"have you no shame?"

Mrs. Lovecome considered. After a pause she shook her head.

"No," she said, "at least, I don't think so."

"It is a most dreadful thing, an unmistakable judgment from Heaven," said Doctor Pressire sombrely, sitting down and putting his legs straight out in front of him and pushing his lips up, "that we should have met thus, in this place, in the presence of the fruit of—the fruit of——"

"If you mean Beatrice, I *do* think she's a pet!" cried Mrs. Lovecombe. "Oh, Harrovius, it *was* unkind of you—I don't mean to be nasty, but you *were* mean—to go off and leave me in that attic in Heidelberg like you did!"

"I was offered a high academic position," said Dr. Pressure stiffly, "in which you——"

"It's rather like Alice and Jumbo, isn't it," said Mrs. Lovecome, and she giggled.

"Alice said to Jumbo, I love you;
   Jumbo said to Alice, I don't believe you do—
   'Cos if you really loved me, like you say you do——

you wouldn't go off and take a high academic position, and leave me in an attic in Heidelberg!"

"I see no reason whatsoever to introduce the subject of pachyderms, or to sing vulgar rhymes——"

"Oh, don't you like Alice and Jumbo?"

"I do not wish to discuss Alice and—the pachyderms at all. Merciful heavens, have we both lost our reason? Pray be serious."

"I am serious," protested Mrs. Lovecome. "I'm quite as serious as you are only we have different ways of showing it."

Doctor Pressure stared at the floor.

"And you seemed to love me so much, even that *morning*!" suddenly said Mrs. Lovecome, but not angrily. "You tied my scarf on, as usual, and kissed me. And when I came back from the flower-factory at lunch-time you and Beatrice had *gone*."

Doctor Pressure muttered something about unsuitable influences for the child.

"Now, honestly, Harrovius, if it comes to that, I don't think *you* are a suitable influence. You're ever so much more high-and-mighty than you used to be, and all this going-on about sin, as if we had been up to I-don't-know-what——"

"*High-and-mighty! I-don't-know-what!* Jenny, Jenny—Jane, I should say, have not the bitter years taught you to speak the Queen's English?"

"No, Harrovius, they haven't. The difference is that once I used to cry when you corrected me, and feel cross and hurt; and now I laugh, but oh! I *have* missed you correcting me, these last twenty years."

"Serpent!" exclaimed Doctor Pressure, suddenly standing up and losing the Fifth Silver Sunflower of Sicily, "Temptress! Avaunt!"

"What on earth does *avaunt* mean?" inquired Mrs. Lovecome, unmoved and taking out a little mirror by which she tidied a curl. "I've always wanted to know."

"Begone! Out of my life for ever!"

Mrs. Lovecome replaced the mirror in her reticule and shook her head.

"No, Harrovius. I'm not going to avaunt this time. Thanks to hard work and my own talents I have now a modest but sufficient fortune of my own; I have bought a house in Belgrave Square and established a school and there I intend to stay. I have also seen my daughter, and her boots are shocking and her bonnets a disgrace. Further, I have seen you keeping the young fellows—gentlemen, I should say—off the poor love as if they were flies and you were a whisk not meaning to be vulgar. I love her more every time I see her. And though I don't expect you to believe it," concluded Mrs. Lovecome, shutting her reticule with a snap, "I also love you."

After a pause, in which Doctor Pressure made such faces and sounds as he thought appropriate to the extreme horror, shamelessness, degradation, etc., etc., of the situation, he said hoarsely:

"And what do you mean to do to me and mine?"

"Oh, don't be so daft," said Mrs. Lovecome, furling her fan with a clash. "Beatrice is going to marry Captain Gabriel Venner and you, Harrovius, are going to marry me."

CHAPTER XVI

MEANWHILE, Major Pillichoddie had left the ball at an early hour, and was now sitting in the parlour of The Bugle Blast. He was saying slowly, between sips of hot toddy:

". . . And the theodolite registered 47·9 degrees Centigrade, making an allowance for the angle of two degrees induced by the gradient of the bluff upon which we had taken—ah—cover. It will be clear to you, no doubt, what our problem was."

Bella, who was trimming a bonnet with jet bugles, nodded.

"Should we rely upon the theodolite, which indicated the height of the bluff, and reckon upon our personal experience of how many breaths a dacoit inhales and exhales per moment, and await their advance, calculating the rate of approach of the dacoits per breath per foot per hour, or should we charge 'em?"

Again Bella nodded.

"And then, at that very moment while we were discussing the problem, what do you think, by George, happened to the theodolite?"

"It broke."

"Quite right! Quite right! But how did you guess?"

"Well, it 'ad been through a lot, Major, in one way and another. Thirty-six hours in that fort place, and then swimmin' that river, and nearly dyin' of thirst afterwards and them blacks pottin' at you be'ind the rocks. I'm not surprised it broke. I would 'ave."

"Yes, it broke. And then"—the Major leant forward and excitedly grasped the bonnet; Bella disengaged it— "our position was perilous, indeed."

"It must 'ave been. You just sit there and drink up your toddy and I'll go out into the bar for a minute, if you'll excuse me. Shan't be long, and I'll 'ear the rest of it when I come back."

She replaced her apron over her handsome dress and hurried to the door, where the head and shoulders of Dannit, beckoning eagerly, could be discerned near the curtain. The Major continued to gaze into the fire.

"Well, young gentlemen, and what can I do for you?" she inquired in no gentle voice, pulling the curtain to. "'Urry up, I'm sittin' with a friend."

"Bella, my queen of hearts, how would you like to marry Major Pillichoddie?" said Cussett in an excited whisper.

Bella looked at him steadily.

"You're not the first that's said that to me," she answered at length.

"Well, why not?" broke in Dannit. "A gentleman—in close touch with the Queen—a fine fortune——"

"Fine fortune, has he?" interrupted Bella quickly. "Then what's he doing sitting in the private room at The Bugle Blast, I'd like to know? I thought he was broke to the wide."

"He likes your company, my love, that's what!"

"Oh, he's a strange fellow, always alone, none of us have much to do with him except occasionally the

Colonel," said Dannit carelessly. "Perhaps he feels his solitary state at times—I don't know."

Bella nodded.

"Ah, pore gentleman. Gets lonely like. We all know what that is," and she made herself draw a deep sigh. Her face was red and excited.

"It would be a charity to marry him, indeed."

"Stop his boozing. Bring a woman's touch into his life," muttered Bella, pulling the black fringe on her gown. "But there's one little drawback, young gents. The Major hasn't asked me. He don't say nothing admiring or personal, you know. Just talks about fightin' them blacks all the time, and I listens and says yes and no and fancy that."

"More than any of us do," laughed Cussett, who was leaning against the wall swinging his cap to and fro.

"If the Major were properly boozed up he wouldn't know whether he'd asked you or not," said Cussett persuasively. "Father Doogood would marry you, for the good of your two souls, and in ten minutes you'd be Mrs. Pillichoddie, the Major's lady!"

Bella stared from one to the other in silence for a moment; then she observed:

"You're up to something."

"Quite right, my charmer; we are. You've rumbled us. But not a word!"

"How can I say a word when I don't know what it's about?"

"All—you've—got—to—do—is—to—marry—the—Major," said Dannit, bending forward and digging his finger ten times into her plump shoulder. "Once it's done, you can't be a loser by it——"

"I'll see I'm not!" said Bella fiercely, shaking the terrible barley-sugar curls. "And my brother, Sam Badd, 'ull see to it, too!"

"Capital!" cried Dannit, slapping her on the back. "That's agreed, then?"

Bella nodded slowly; her broad red face was determined and her eyes widely opened.

"Now get some of your oldest—what's the Major's favourite tipple?" asked Cussett, who had fallen into a fever of triumphant glances and excitement.

"Brandy."

"Get up some of the Napoleon; I'll pay for it. And I'll go get Father Doogood to come in. Bella, do you ply the Major with the brandy. Gad——" muttered Cussett, hurrying away, "the pleasure gardens are as good as lost to those poor devils of waiters at this moment!"

.   .   .   .   .

Major Pillichoddie, without knowing he did so, sighed as he sat up in bed in his frilled nightshirt, sipping whisky-and-water and glancing over *The Times*. The thought that to-day would be a trying one did not consciously darken the morning, for duty was with the Major so much a habit that it was automatic and never called forth the suspicion of a grumble; nevertheless, he sighed.

It was the day of his monthly visit to the Palace with General Ramm's recipe. Major Milde and Lieutenant Toloreaux were to accompany him.

While his servant was preparing his bath, Major Pillichoddie took out the ancient Hindoo carved boxes that contained the precious recipes, and looked for one that should please and interest the Queen. The bills for the Club were even heavier than was customary this month, and it must be an unusually good one, to placate her.

"Hullo, Pillichoddie," said Major Milde diffidently, coming into the room in full dress. "Your man let me in. I thought perhaps you wouldn't mind. I'm ready early."

"Not at all. Sit down. Just going to have my bath." He continued to hunt in the recipe box.

Major Milde sat down.

"I had a letter from Georgiana and the girls this morning," he said, with a brightening of his expression.

"Indeed. *How to remove dark patches from brown boots.* We've had that. Hey, damme."

"Yes."

"How are they all? Well, I trust?"

Major Milde looked dashed.

"Emily and Honoria have had nervous chills. Amelia and Agnes and Agatha have not been well, either, Susan's and Tabiatha's headaches are frequent."

"None of 'em engaged yet?" said the Major rather spitefully: he was apt to vent his ill-humour. "*The stopper of a scent-bottle, if it be obdurately jammed, may be*—no, that won't do."

Major Milde's face brightened once more.

"Amelia and Susan are. They're getting married this autumn."

"Let me see, Amelia and Susan have each got a thousand pounds, have they not?"

Major Milde nodded.

"Not much, but it helps," observed Major Pillichoddie.

"It always grieves me so much that the question of money should enter into it at all," said Major Milde gently. "They are all such dear, good girls. Love should be enough."

"Pshaw," said Major Pillichoddie, absently. "Ah— what have we here? *It is a common fallacy to suppose that when washing vegetables*—this looks more promising."

His servant came in. "Sir, the bath is ready."

"Ah! this will do! Very well, Pound, I am coming now."

He went into the bedroom and Major Milde sat and stared out of the window at the early autumn trees, with the smoke of the first of the two cigars he daily allowed himself wreathing slowly about his ineffectual features.

Major Pillichoddie's temper grew steadily worse on the ride to the Palace. He was annoyed by that fellow Toloreaux's face, as pink as a woman's, by George; and that fellow Milde, gassing about his dear Georgiana and the girls; Gad, we might be Miss Sopp's Academy out for an airing and done with it. Thank Gad I was never fool enough to marry. Softens a feller.

On their ride through the grounds towards the Palace they passed Doctor Pressure, striding along in what was evidently much distress of mind and muttering to himself. Their horses would have ridden him down had not Major Pillichoddie bawled at him and caused him to leap aside.

"Feller's brain must be goin'. All his what-you-may-callums and books and stuff have turned his head," commented Major Pillichoddie furiously.

The ritual at the Palace was always the same; the two officers in attendance on Major Pillichoddie stood at attention outside the Queen's apartments while he read aloud to her the recipe of the month. Then, after a few gracious remarks from his sovereign, the Major retired.

To-day, Ticky and Major Milde took up their position outside the long white folding doors with the panels and handles painted with pansies and wild roses, and Major Pillichoddie, standing at attention, was announced by the huge footman as the doors were flung wide. The two officers caught a glimpse, amid the gold and crimson stateliness of the room, of a small stout figure dressed in magenta satin with some bright Berlin woolwork in one hand, and a slender figure all in white seated beside it. Then the doors closed, and the two officers, knowing that they were safe for the next quarter of an hour, stood at ease and glanced about them.

"Miss Beatrice is on duty to-day, I see," observed Lieutenant Toloreaux. "How I wish we could smoke."

"A charming creature; she is not unlike my fourth daughter, Amelia."

"How are all the gir—the Misses Milde, Major? Well, I trust?"

"Moderately well, I thank you. I fear the air of Devonshire is a little relaxing for them."

"I regret to hear it," murmured Ticky, going off into a day-dream about the rosy earth and blue seas of that lovely place; and both were silent.

In the quietness, the reverent hush of the very air that filled the lofty corridors and chambers of the Palace, a voice, muffled slightly by distance, suddenly began to sound. Ticky lifted his head, nodded and smiled. It was the voice of Major Pillichoddie, beginning to read aloud the household hint.

CHAPTER XVII

LIEUTENANT TOLOREAUX and Major Milde listened.

"*It is a common fallacy to suppose that when washing vegetables*—pray, pardon me, Your Majesty," and the voice broke off, and there followed a coughing set-out.

"We trust that you have not a cold, Major Pillichoddie," observed a small, clear, rather severe voice.

"Your Majesty is most gracious; I thank Your Majesty and am happy to say that it was no more than what is known among the humbler section of Your Majesty's subjects as a frog-in-the-throat. I will, with Your Majesty's permission, resume. Ahem."

"Pray do so, Major Pillichoddie. You have our attention."

"*It is a common fallacy to suppose that when washing vegetables the casting of a handful of common salt into the water will cause the various insect pests which infest the plants to forsake their lairs and be driven out into the water.*"

Here the Major suddenly paused. It was evident to both listeners, who were straining their ears with the keenest attention, that the Queen was looking at him inquiringly.

"*Fallacy*, Major Pillichoddie?" said the small severe voice.

A pause, while the Major evidently consulted the paper. Then he said:

"That is what it says, Your Majesty."

"You may continue," said the Queen, after another pause. The listeners, who knew how much depended upon her favourable reception of the hint, were by now exchanging alarmed glances.

"*This is not so*," continued the Major, in a much less confident voice. "*Salt will only serve to drive the insect pests back into their lairs, whence it will be difficult if not impossible to dislodge them.*"

Then there was silence.

It was broken by a chilly laugh from the Queen.

"Ha, ha. Very excellent, Major Pillichoddie. Most amusing, indeed. Nevertheless, as we ride with Lord Melbourne in an hour and are pressed for time, we desire you to read to us immediately the other hint."

"The—the other hint, Your Majesty?"

"Certainly, Major Pillichoddie. We had thought that we made ourselves sufficiently plain. We mean the hint that is not intended to be a jest."

"There—may it please Your Majesty, there is no other hint."

"No other hint, Major Pillichoddie?"

"None, Ma'am. That is to say——"

"And this, that you have just read aloud to us, is taken from General Ramm's collection?"

"I assure Your Majesty——"

"From the boxes from India?"

"Your Majesty——"

There was a sound of skirts rustling sharply as though someone had stood up, and begun to pace up and down.

"It is very upsetting to us, Major Pillichoddie, to think of our millions of loyal subjects in India believing in such nonsense. Every woman in England knows that salt drives insects *out* of cabbages, not *in*. Were the minds of our Indian subjects not darkened by vile superstitions they could not credit such foolishness. We make no doubt that the rumour was put about by Tippoo Sahib."

Here Major Pillichoddie began to cough again, and the Queen said sharply:

"Surely you have a rheum, Major Pillichoddie? Are your brother officers similarly afflicted?"

"Most of 'em have coughs, Your Majesty." The Major's voice was very sulky; suddenly its direction changed, as if he had turned to look at somebody other than the Queen, and it sounded spiteful. "Especially Captain Gabriel Venner, Your Majesty. Captain Venner's cough is the worst of them all; shouldn't wonder if it proved fatal. Those large tall fellers often go off suddenly, Your Majesty."

"Now what could be Tippoo's *reason* for putting about the rumour, which would discourage our loyal Indian subjects from using salt?" The Queen was evidently still pacing up and down, and her voice was thoughtful.

"May I make a suggestion, Your Majesty?"

"(No, Major Pillichoddie, you may not.) We must speak to Lord Melbourne about it. Utter rubbish! We are *surprised*, Major Pillichoddie, that you should have ventured to bring such a piece of foolishness to our notice."

"Perhaps it was only that one Hindoo, Your Majesty, who believed it," said Major Pillichoddie glumly.

"To which Hindoo do you refer, Major Pillichoddie?"

"The one who gave General Ramm the hints and recipes, Your Majesty."

"Then if that be so, the man was not in his right senses and all his other observations are valueless," retorted the Queen sharply. "Did it not strike you, Major Pillichoddie, as rubbish when you originally read it?"

"I know nothing of domestic matters, Ma'am."

"That is very plain to see, from the size of the bills at the Club," said the Queen awfully, and Major Milde and Lieutenant Toloreaux, who had been listening with extreme alarm and concern, exchanged glances of horror.

Here there was a low murmur; someone was speaking, but they could not distinguish the words.

"Yes, yes, child," said the Queen, "but do not be long; I want my wool wound."

A moment later, and the doors were swung open by the footman, and Ticky and Major Milde just caught a glimpse of the Queen, very red in the face, and Major Pillichoddie, standing at attention and very purple, before Miss Pressure hurried out, a flying wraith in white.

As the doors shut behind her, she paused for a moment and put her hand on Ticky's arm and looked up earnestly into his face.

"Lieutenant Toloreaux, it is very bold of me—I fear you will think me unwomanly——"

"Never, Miss Beatrice," Ticky said with his kindest smile.

"Oh, then, thank you, I will go and fetch it——" and away she hurried, her crinoline swaying along the crimson carpeted corridor, between the marble busts of dead statesmen, past the huge dark pictures framed in gold, like an enormous white harebell.

Major Milde and Ticky had barely time to exchange a few agitated words about the situation (the Queen's voice could still be heard censuring Major Pillichoddie) before

Beatrice had returned, and was pressing into Ticky's hand a small bottle wrapped in pink tissue paper.

"It is black currant cordial," she murmured, "for Captain Venner's cough. The—the welfare of the Regiment is always present in my thoughts, and—and—I do not like to think of any of—of the officers . . . anything happening to any of them."

"My dear Miss Beatrice," said Lieutenant Toloreaux tenderly, venturing to take her hand in his, while Major Milde took the other and began to pat it, "we appreciate your thought for us very deeply, and I can assure you that when I give this cordial to Captain Gabriel he will be the happiest man between here and Aldershot."

"And his cough—is it indeed so troublesome?" faltered Beatrice.

"Oh, he has a slight cough, but it is nothing like so serious as Major Pillichoddie makes out, and the moment that he receives your gentle gift I know he will be cured."

"Thank you—oh, thank you."

"He is such a good fellow," Ticky went on, softly and persuasively, "the dearest of fellows, I assure you."

"I—I am sure of it." Beatrice gently withdrew her hand, not meeting his earnest gaze. "I must go back now, I told Her Majesty that I wanted to fetch a handkerchief." The doors opened once more and she hurriedly re-entered the Royal apartment.

"Deuced touching," muttered Major Milde, blowing his nose.

"Gad, Gabriel will be in Paradise!" murmured Ticky, gazing delightedly at the little bottle and executing a jig. "Would that all might come right for him in that quarter."

At this moment the doors were flung wide; Major Pillichoddie bowed himself out backwards from the Queen, who was sitting upright and doing Berlin woolwork very fast and not looking at him.

Then the doors shut again.

Major Pillichoddie's aspect was so fearful that both gentlemen refrained from addressing him on the ride back to the Club.

．　　　．　　　．　　　．　　　．

More trouble awaited Major Pillichoddie on arriving at his quarters.

Usually, on his return from his monthly interview with the Queen, he was in a pleasant mood due to duty being done; he relaxed; he smoked a cigar and glanced through *The Clipper* before changing his clothes in readiness for luncheon alone with the Colonel, who naturally must always have a report of how the interview with the Queen had progressed.

But when he entered his chambers on this morning, they appeared to be full of people: there was his servant, Pound, and Cussett and Dannit, the two ensigns; and a large ill-favoured fellow whom he recognized as Badd, Molloy's servant, and—Gad, what in the name of all that was infuriating were *they* doing here?—that woman from The Bugle Blast and that parson feller, Toogood, or some such name, looking deuced down in the mouth. Pound, who was greatly agitated, was pushing 'em all into a corner and they were all talking at once.

"'Egad, what the devil is going on here?" shouted the Major.

Then everybody began to talk louder than ever.

"Ahem! Just looked in to inquire after your health, sir."

"Oh, Major, don't you remember what happened last night?"

"Don't want to make no trouble, sir, but I'm 'ere to see my sister done right by."

"I did try to get 'em all to go 'ome, sir, but it was 'opeless——"

"If ye'll be afther having a word with me in privit, Major, I can put the matter right in a moment——"

"I've got me lines, Major—here they are——" and Bella thrust a paper at Major Pillichoddie, who snatched it and flung it on the fire.

"Merciful 'eavens! Me lines!"

"I don't care what they were—get out of here, all of you, immediately!" thundered the Major, shooing everybody towards the door. "Cussett and Dannit, consider yourselves under arrest. You, Madam, what's your name, get out of here, back to your public-house. Father Toogood, I don't want you to put anything right—there's nothing wrong that I know of——"

" 'Twas only a bit of a jhoke, Major—done to please the bits of bhoys. I left out the most important part. 'Tis not really married at all ye aren't——"

"Of course I'm not married!" bellowed the Major. "Are you all raving mad? Begone, all of you. Not another word! Here, Pound, give me a hand"—and the Major set his shoulder against the door and began slowly to close it upon the protesting mob—"Badd, you're on a charge. Inform Lieutenant Molloy so. Now, Pound —together! Heave!"

Slowly the door was pressed home; the latch clicked and the Major turned the key. Then he leant back against it, panting. For a few moments there was a babble of voices outside, and then they gradually grew fainter as the speakers retreated, and at last there was quiet.

"I 'umbly apologize, sir," began Pound, who was pale with horror. "I was just a-laying out of your trousers when——"

"Yes, yes, that will do, I don't wish to hear any more about it; get me dressed at once," said Major Pillichoddie irritably; and Badd, reflecting not without regret that there wasn't another officer in the Regiment with as little natural curiosity as his Major, proceeded to do as he was told.

And Major Pillichoddie put the incident out of his mind.

It did not seem to him to affect the welfare of the Regiment, and he had the experienced soldier's habit of dismissing what he regarded as irrelevancies. If Cussett, Dannit and Badd were insolent they could be punished and this he had done. If Bella and Father Toogood or whatever he called himself had gone mad, so much the worse for them, but it was nothing to do with the Major. Bella existed, in the evenings, as an ear; by day, she was not. The Major settled his coat, and gloomily drank some brandy. He was very cut up, deuced worried in fact, about his interview with the Queen. And in a few moments he would have to face the Colonel.

CHAPTER XVIII

THE sounds of a harp greeted Major Pillichoddie as he entered the Colonel's private room. The Colonel, having spent a stimulating morning riding his charger at full gallop towards a line of troops and then pulling it up within two inches of them and putting them on a charge if they flinched, was now lying relaxed upon an amber velvet sofa smoking a narghile, and listening, with half-shut eyes, to Major Milde's rendering of "The Harp That Once Through Tara's Halls." Major Milde, who was sitting behind the Colonel and out of his sight, was looking exceedingly miserable.

Major Pillichoddie saluted; but the Colonel did not immediately lift his long eyelashes, and when he did so he gave Major Pillichoddie a cold look and merely sketched a salute.

"Ah, Pillich . . ." he murmured, as if it were too much trouble to say the name.

Major Pillichoddie, without the Colonel's permission, was unable to sit down, so he remained standing. The Colonel continued to draw at his Turkish pipe. Major Milde continued to play the harp and look miserable. Some moments passed.

"Sing, Milde!" suddenly commanded the Colonel. "Let us have some verses in praise of the married state!" and he darted a glance of purest fury at Major Pillichoddie, who rocked slightly but made no other sign that he had seen it.

Major Milde obediently lifted up a fine, if surprising, bass:

> " 'Tis sweet to wander o'er the dales
> In the morning tide of life,
> But sweeter far
> By light of star
> To fondle a loving wife!
> 'Tis sweet to ride o'er dale and hill,
> To scale the mountain crest
> But sweeter far
> By light of star
> To lie on a tender breast!
> A ten-der breast—
> A ten——"

"Bah!" suddenly exclaimed the Colonel, dashing down his pipe. "Enough!"

Major Milde, stopped. Out of the corner of his eye Major Pillichoddie observed him wipe his forehead, and then launch a stealthy kick towards the harp.

"So, Major Pillichoddie," went on the Colonel, sitting upright and looking steadily at him, "you are married."

"No, I am not, sir," replied the Major crossly, but relieved that the Colonel's obvious irritation with him was due to no more than a misunderstanding. "I suppose there has been some kind of a jest going about. Those two puppies, Cussett and Dannit, seem to be at the bottom of it. I'm sure I don't know half of what it's about. I put each of them under arrest and thought no more of the matter."

"A woman named . . . Bella . . . I believe, of The Bugle Blast tavern," said the Colonel distastefully, examining his narghile, "is concerned in the matter?"

"I really cannot say, sir," returned Major Pillichoddie with some indifference. "She was certainly at my rooms this morning and apparently far gone in insanity, but——"

"By what right did she come to your rooms?" demanded the Colonel.

"By no right, sir. She——"

"Have you been frequenting The Bugle Blast and her company?"

"I'm blest if I can say," roared Major Pillichoddie, losing his small patience. "I may have spoken to the creature once or twice but as for——"

"It does not suit well, Major Pillichoddie, with the dignity of an officer in the First Bloods to frequent the society of barmaids."

"I have *not* frequented her society, sir!"

"Major Pillichoddie, you have been seen there night after night. Sitting by the fire. In the private parlour. Gossiping with this—this——"

"Oh lord, well, maybe I have, maybe I have. What of it? No doubt I was in my cups and wanted someone to talk to. No harm is done."

The Colonel sank back upon the sofa and rang a silver bell. A servant entered.

"Serve luncheon now. There will be myself and"—the Colonel's voice lingered over the words—"Lieutenant Molloy. Send someone to fetch him. Now, Milde; you must bid farewell to your beloved harp for a few hours. We shall meet again this evening, gentlemen. Good morning." He was half-way out of the room when Major Pillichoddie, stunned by the breaking of the habit of his monthly luncheon alone with the Colonel, a ritual of some fifteen years' duration, burst out:

"But, sir, I wish to give you a report of my interview with Her Majesty this morning. It is most vitally important."

"Write it," said the Colonel, without turning round, and lounged gracefully from the room.

Major Milde and Major Pillichoddie stared at one another.

"You are out of favour, now, I fear," said the latter gently. Then he shook the harp and added: "*Blow* this instrument."

Major Pillichoddie said in a dazed tone: "After fifteen years. And the Queen is angered with me, too. Upon my soul, I feel as if I should go mad, Milde. What is it all about? One moment all is clear as daylight; my duty, my plans, everything, and the next moment—I am not boozed, am I, Milde?"

"No, my dear old Pillichoddie, you are perfectly sober. But I fear that you are the victim of a plot."

"A plot, Milde?"

"Ay; a plot to get you out of favour with the Colonel, so that you shall lose your influence with him."

"But why, Milde, why?"

"So that you shall no longer be able to oppose his plan to obtain the waiters' pleasure gardens."

"But this is monstrous, Milde! General Ramm—our revered founder—gave those poor devils—why, everybody knows—hey, damme—it's all written down in their Charter—why should the Colonel—I thought I'd talked him out of all that rubbish—more like Napoleon Bonaparte than the Colonel of an English regiment—foreign non-sense—tyrannical—why, it's disgraceful, Milde, and I told him so!"

"Exactly," nodded Major Milde. "And as you are so strongly opposed to his plan, those who wish to curry favour with him have plotted to get you out of his favour. And I fear they have succeeded."

"Well, that can't be helped, damme," said Major Pillichoddie testily. "No doubt that will all come right, silly feller. But those poor devils—no, Milde. It mustn't happen. They have their rights; it's all they *have* got, and by God they shall keep 'em! or my name is not Hugo Pillichoddie!"

"Splendid! I am with you!" cried Major Milde, and as the two officers clasped hands enthusiastically and made to hasten from the room, he tripped over the harp and fell flat on his face.

CHAPTER XIX

IF nothing has so far been said of the Men, who made up the regiment, that is because they were always so busy drilling or doing fatigues that they had no spare time in which anything could happen to them that is worth recording.

A high standard, naturally, was expected of them. The nails on the soles of their boots had to be so highly polished that they were capable of heliographing a message three miles on a dull day and ten miles on a sunny one. Their bo'sun's whistles had to be so bright as to cause officers to blink twice on seeing them.

The official name for the bo'sun's whistle was the Back Tag. It consisted of a small length of white cord, attached to the back of each man's collar, and terminating in a small metal cone resembling a shoe-lace end. This was made of brass, and it had to be polished, and the cord to be pipeclayed, while the man was wearing his coat, with his hands behind his back. This was not an easy task. It was part of the daily routine and was imposed for purposes of discipline. The name bo'sun's whistle originated in a remark once made by Private Beer in the days of General Ramm, when first the back tags were issued: "Crikey! these here things is about as much use to us chaps as a bo'sun's whistle."

There were a number of sayings of Private Beer extant among the Men. He had remained a private all his life, being degraded from the rank of corporal no less than three hundred and seventeen times. "After all, somebody 'as to be privates," was one of his sayings, which did something to comfort those who had failed to rise above that status.

Friendship between the Men and the waiters was not encouraged by the officers, because it was suspected that when they got together they compared notes; nevertheless, a certain amount of social intercourse did take place; and on the afternoon after Major Pillichoddie's fall from the Colonel's favour some of the waiters and Men were gathered together round Mrs. Sawyer's shrimpery, smoking and gossiping.

On the other side of the Club, below the South Tower, was a garden embellished with every rare tree and shrub that a heavy purse and an informed taste could provide, as well as smooth lawns, a conservatory and hothouses, where lady visitors could wander and admire the showy begonia and the exotic geranium. This afternoon the regimental band was playing, and tea was being served on the lawn, under a sky of delicate blue penetrated by the lazy yet fierce rays of a late autumn sun. Some magnificent oaks and beeches already wore the splendours of the declining year; beneath them the ladies were sitting, among them Lady Venner and Mrs. Lovecome with Beatrice. Doctor Pressure had got as far as the middle of the lawn and then seen Mrs. Lovecome (who cheerfully waved her parasol at him) and gone rushing back as if he had forgotten to turn off the oven. Beatrice, after some hesitation, had timidly approached and been affectionately greeted by Mrs. Lovecome, at whose side she was now seated, surveying the beautiful scene.

The sombre purple uniforms of the officers as they moved against the tawny branches and freshly watered green lawns contrasted pleasingly with the scarlet of the mess-orderlies' jackets, the scarlet of the geraniums in their beds, the delicate dresses of the ladies glimmering under the shade of the trees. And those masses of gold, of russet, leaves! boldly reared against the drowsy blue of the sky! A thousand wasps droned above the preserve pots, and the mess-orderlies were kept busy flapping at them and muttering to each other that this was worse nor the Crimea.

"Who made your gown, love?" presently inquired Mrs. Lovecome of Beatrice, "Worth?"

"Oh, no——"

"I thought not." Mrs. Lovecome shut her eyes for a moment, as was her habit when she disapproved of anything; then opened them again and let them rest idly upon Lieutenant Molloy, who happened to be passing. He sat down abruptly upon a Madras chair.

"——A local dressmaker, a pious and humble Christian, who ekes out a living by such work," concluded Beatrice.

"Just what I suspected," said Mrs. Lovecome amiably. "Tell me, is your papa going to join us presently?"

"I am not sure—he felt a little faint, I think—he was with me a moment since but went back to the house. Perhaps I ought——"

"Oh, do not leave this delicious shade; I will go and find him myself: I should like to ask his advice upon a little matter of business," and Mrs. Lovecome stood up, unfurling her parasol, which was of pale pink lace. She was dressed in lilac silk thinly striped with black and her bonnet was smothered in dark red carnations. "That is his study window, is it not?" and she nodded towards the Club. "No—pray do not trouble to show me—I will explore."

And she strode gracefully away. As she drew near to him, Lieutenant Molloy rose unsteadily to his feet, holding on to the back of the Madras chair, and prepared to address her.

At the same instant a large shadow loomed over Beatrice and Lady Venner, and a voice said: "Aw—how de do, Aunt. How de do, Miss Beatwice. I was wonderin', Aunt, Miss Beatwice—if—if you would care to see the conservatowy? They say there is a gweat lily in a pond there, don't you know, as big as a dining-woom table. Most instwuctive."

"I am too old for lilies," said Lady Venner with a pleasant smile, "but do you go with Captain Venner, my dear, and come back in half an hour and tell me all about it."

"Oh yes—it would be delightful—but Papa—I believe he is not feeling——"

"Mrs. Lovecome will take care of Doctor Pressure," said Lady Venner firmly, who knew all Mrs. Lovecome's plans and heartily approved them. "You go and study the lily: it is a unique opportunity."

So slowly, side by side, Captain Gabriel and Beatrice moved away.

"Madame Jeanne——" said Barry, hoarsely; then cleared his throat, silently cursing.

"Ah, Lieutenant Molloy! How do you do?"

"I am—well, I thank you. I—hope you are well, too."

"I am always well," smiled Mrs. Lovecome.

"N-naturally. One does not expect Venus—Venus to be out of sorts."

Venus! Well, I'm blessed, thought Mrs. Lovecome, looking at him with large brown eyes that gave away nothing. He's one of the ask-you-the-same-evening kind.

She said kindly:

"Thank you; how pretty."

"Madame Jeanne," stammered Barry, beginning to walk beside her across the lawn, "pray forgive what must seem an extraordinary impertinence—put it down to—to —what you will—but would you do me the honour of—of dining with me one evening? *This* evening?"

"I do not dine alone with gentlemen," she answered pleasantly, "but I shall be pleased to see you on any Thursday at four o'clock at my house, 24 Belgrave Square."

"Of course. Yes—thank you, I shall be charmed, most honoured," he muttered, feeling ill with disappointment; and for a moment they continued to walk in silence.

It *is* queer the way they always know, mused Mrs. Lovecome. I've got the right manner—well, usually the right manner—the right friends, the right address—and *still* they always know. It's my nose or something. Ladies have noses that turn down, and smaller eyes.

She turned on Barry a smile that made him stagger.

"I must leave you here; I have to see Doctor Pressure on business."

"Oh, business. Oh—yes. You—you said I might come on Thursday. May I not come before?"

"Well——"

"To-morrow?"

"No; I really think Thursday would be better," said Mrs. Lovecome firmly, though with another smile, and passed on into the cool rooms of the Club. She regretted having to refuse his invitation, for her tastes inclined to the supper-party rather than the tea-party, but what sense was there in running into Trouble with a capital T?

Barry, dismayed at his own weakness but unable to resist temptation, sat down on a chair near the porch in hopes of seeing her emerge later.

In the conservatory, the young plants stood up tender yet vigorous in the light pouring through the clear glass. The warm air smelled of geranium leaves, and all down the vista, roofed by a long glass dome, was a pattern of fragile green leaves, scarlet or pink flowers, water-cans and flower-pots and benches. At the far end something creamy and unbelievably large glimmered amid green leaves on water.

"There it is," murmured Beatrice.

"Miss Beatwice," said Captain Gabriel earnestly, pausing for a moment in the shadow of a giant aspidistra, "I cannot let this opportunity pass without sayin' how vewy, vewy happy the little bottle of black-cuwwant cordial made me."

"So afraid you would think me unwomanly——" she murmured, trembling.

"Dearwest——" Captain Gabriel paused; Beatrice did not dare to lift her eyes. "Miss Beatwice, your gentle gift, your care for my welfare, gave me hope. I—I had not dared to hope, until now. *Is* there hope, Miss Beatwice?"

She very slightly inclined her head. She could not speak. Captain Gabriel gently took her little hand, in its pale glove, and lifted it to his lips.

"Dearwest—Miss Beatwice."

"It is—you will understand, Captain Venner, that while Papa needs me his health is my first care."

"Of course, dearwest—Miss Beatwice. That is fully understood. But I *may* hope! Ah, if you knew how happy you have made me!"

"I, too, am very happy, Captain Venner." She gave him a shy upward smile from her blue eyes. "And now I think we had best go and look at the lily, do not you?"

CHAPTER XX

THERE were as many rumours flying about as there were wasps. The Queen, it was reported, was much concerned at news of fresh disturbances in India; and one of the officers, it was not exactly known which, had offended the Colonel by an imprudent liaison. And there was also a feeling of excitement in the air, due partly to the wasps but partly to a less obvious cause; groups of officers stood talking earnestly together; and the mess-orderlies all had very long faces, but of course nobody troubled to look at *them*.

George Licker had got himself up in his best suit, and with a contemptuous permission obtained from the Mess-Sergeant, was gliding among the company, proffering cup and ices and listening.

"Puts me in mind of a cloves-moff's egg," said the Mess-Sergeant, Cannonroyal, gloomily to one of the orderlies. "'Taint so much 'is face; it's 'is way of goin' on. Soap, tallow, and cloves-moffs' eggs. If we 'adn't been so short-'anded what with so many of you articles being C.B., I'd never 'ave let 'im in."

George was at this moment approaching near, without seeming obviously to do so, to the Colonel, who was talking to a very old retired general, a cousin of no less a person than the founder, General Ramm. Slim and gorgeous, drooping beneath his load of copper lace—yet how erect he could stand on parade!—the Colonel listened with half-closed eyes and a dying look while the old general, who was not at all deaf and still passionately interested in the Regiment in which he had once served, asked him questions.

George, approaching, heard a loud droning voice uttering the words: "Tippoo Sahib . . . salt mines at Nangpany . . . situation revealed by a simple domestic incident . . . ha . . . not unlike that of the *grease*, which led up to the recent disastrous events . . . Her Majesty . . . Tippoo Sahib's motives. . . ."

Silently George held a glass brimming with golden liquid and bruised fruit under the Colonel's pinched waxen nose. The Colonel almost snatched at it and drained it; George had another ready before the first was empty and handed it without being asked. The Colonel gave him a piercing yet approving glance as he drank off the second beaker; and, taking advantage of the fact that the old General was also drinking some cup, said rapidly in a low tone:

"Find Lieutenant Molloy at once and tell him to await me in the Chapel. Also find out where Lieutenant Toloreaux is and report his whereabouts to me."

"Oh, sir, begging your pardon, Lieutenant Toloreaux is in the Pleasure Gardens, the Waiters' Pleasure Gardens, sir, with Miss Sawyer," whispered George, almost overcome at his success.

The Colonel looked stern and disgusted, and the old General coming at this moment out of his beaker, which he set down on the tray with a bang, the two strolled off together. George darted away to find Lieutenant Molloy, and after an unsuccessful search among the groups strolling over the lawns and under the trees, found himself opposite one of the numerous entrances to the Club. Here was seated Beatrice's maid, Sour.

She was sheltered from the sunlight by a large old umbrella and while sewing buttons on a nightshirt intended for the Caffres was occasionally glancing sharply across at Beatrice and showing her disapproval of the gay tune the band was playing, the number of men about, etc., by small apprehensive shakings of the head and compressings of the lips. As George approached, she hastily bundled the nightshirt together in order that Lord Melbourne, who was now strolling past with the Colonel some fifty

feet away might not see what it was; and gave the youth
a severe look.

"Beggin' your pardon, ma'am," and George took off
his hat, "but have you see Lieutenant Molloy about
anywheres?"

Sour poked her head out from under the umbrella and
then silently pointed with her needle towards the back of
a Madras chair at some distance away: a walking-out cap
on some dark red curls could just be seen above it. The
owner's eyes were turned towards the door immediately
opposite.

"Led on, but no doubt willingly," said Sour, going
back into the shade of the umbrella once more.

"Thank you, ma'am," said George, bowing. "I won't
keep you from your blessed work of charity no longer,
ma'am. Might I be so bold as to inquire what is the nature
of it, ma'am?"

"It's for the Caffres," muttered Sour, scrubbling the
nightshirt even closer together. "A garment."

"Indeed, ma'am? Oh, what a fortunate people they
are, with so many ladies a-wearin' their fingers to the
bone for them!"

"And never so much as a thank-you, the ungrateful
monkeys," said Sour, thawing slightly.

"Ah, there's not much gratitude in this world, is there,
ma'am?"

"No, nor safety, nor peace, neither."

"You speak quite right, ma'am. And I'm sure everything's done for people, nowadays. Why, my Pa, Mr.
Licker, was a-saying to me only yesterday he'd heard of
some—some—garments intended to be worn after the
sun has set, ma'am, asking your parden for mentioning
such a subject—being made for the Siamese with *frills*
on 'em, ma'am."

Sour gave a disapproving shake of her head but kept her

eyes fixed upon her work, and George, feeling that he had gone too far, was abashed.

In the pause, a murmur of pleasure and interest began to arise from the elegant crowd dispersed about the gardens; ladies came out from the shade and pointed upwards with their parasols; officers sent the orderlies running to fetch their glasses. A balloon had sailed into view above the trees.

Round, soft, and gentle as a pearl, it moved steadily across the blue sky: the ladies had drunk a second cup of tea before at last it faded into the sunny distance and the murmur—so approving, so affectionate—died away.

"Ah, there's no safety anywhere, nowadays," pronounced Sour, compressing her lips towards the place where the balloon had faded, "except in your bed." After a moment's reflection she muttered, "And not always there."

George had bowed to her, and was now hastening away towards the Madras chair.

It was with feelings confused to anguish that Barry received the Colonel's command.

Ambition and desire, those tigers' among the passions, fought furiously within him. But ambition won, and the habits of duty and discipline assisted the sterner feeling. He rose, and without one glance towards the door whence Mrs. Lovecome might reappear, walked away towards the Chapel.

It is damnable luck, thought the young man, striding over the lawns, through the gay music that floated on the air, towards the sacred edifice. What have I done that this should happen to me? Without a ceaseless effort of the will, that exhausted him through his lack of experience in exercising it, he found it impossible to think of anything but Mrs. Lovecome. Intrigue, diplomacy, duty, greed— all feelings and activities were subordinated to this *enchantment.* He groaned and gritted his teeth; he felt as if invisible ropes were pulling him back towards her, but he pushed open the door and went into the Chapel.

Meanwhile the Colonel was saying severely to Major Milde:

"I am sorry, Milde, if the health of your daughter—Miss——"

"Emily, sir."

"Miss Emily is occasioning you anxiety, but you must realize that these constant requests on your part for leave are most irregular."

"I do, indeed, sir, and——"

"You have had no less than a fortnight's leave in the last three months."

Major Milde was silent.

"Have you nothing to say?"

"Only that the delicate health of Mrs. Milde and the gir—and of the Misses Milde unfortunately requires my frequent presence at home, sir. We cannot help our physical constitutions."

"But we can at least try to avoid their interfering with our duties," said the Colonel disagreeably, glancing towards the Chapel. "Well, I suppose you must go. You may take three days."

"You are more than good, sir."

"Oh, well, Milde, curse it, I am not without feelings. Indeed, I am more sensitive than most of you fellows, with your cigars and gaieties; that is my trouble. How are your financial anxieties nowadays with regard to the Misses Milde?"

"Oh, ah, better, I thank you, sir. Honoria, Agatha and Agnes have recently received legacies from two aged aunts and a venerable distant cousin to the extent of three thousand pounds."

"That is not much."

"No, but it helps," answered Major Milde diffidently. "They will now have a thousand pounds each."

"Ah, yes, quite so; well, a little money is always an added attraction, especially if a girl be plain. Good day to you, Milde," and the Colonel nodded, and strode away towards the Chapel.

Barry, who had been moodily studying the memorial tablets, stood to attention and saluted as his superior officer entered. The Colonel motioned to him to sit down, and took a seat himself in one of the pews.

"You have heard, of course, that the Regiment is to acquire the piece of land beyond the wood, known, I believe, as the Recreation Grounds?" he began at once.

"Yes, sir." Barry did not know whether the Colonel wanted him to feign ignorance; he was also doubtful about whether to whisper or not. The Chapel door stood half open and over the Colonel's shoulder could be seen a vision of green lawn and motionless bronze trees. Curse it! Barry painfully brought his thoughts to order and fixed his eyes on the Colonel's face.

"I have decided that the bearer of the proclamation of annexation to the tenants shall be yourself," continued the Colonel.

In spite of his suffering, Barry's heart beat faster and he flushed proudly. For a minute his spirit returned to that lost world where his only passion had been ambition.

"I am honoured indeed, sir," he whispered.

"Your progress is by no means unsatisfactory." The Colonel's eyes were half closed as he studied the young man, but the look that shone from them was very keen. "I think that you should go far—perhaps as far as it is possible for a soldier to go. Provided, that is," the Colonel got gracefully to his feet and made some small adjustment in the cuff of his coat without looking at Barry, "provided that your conduct continues to uphold the honour of the Regiment and to comply with its traditions."

Again Barry flushed, but from very different reasons. He had risen when the Colonel did, and now looked fully at that elegant figure, whose gorgeous uniform and pantherine grace were shown to advantage against the monotone stones of the sacred edifice.

"Even in this Regiment," the Colonel went on softly and bitterly, caressing his drooping moustache with one white hand and staring down at a pew cushion, "there have been cases in which officers forgot their duty, contracted low alliances, allowed other passions than the prestige of the Regiment to influence their conduct."

"I shall not be one of them, sir," Barry whispered through clenched teeth; (the Colonel was not troubling to whisper, because he did not believe in God).

"I know that you will not." The Colonel suddenly lifted his almond eyes in a smile full of charm. "Here is the proclamation. You had best take it immediately. I want the matter settled: that piece of land must be turned into a drill ground by Christmas." He held out a piece of parchment with purple ribbons and bronze seals.

"Am I to take an escort, sir?"

"Yes. Take twelve men. And go at once."

Barry saluted, the Colonel did likewise, and strode out of the Chapel.

.   .   .

"Sergeant Cannonroyal!"

Sergeant Cannonroyal, who had been expecting this, dropped the newspaper he had been swatting wasps with, and saluted and stood to attention.

"Bring twelve men to the edge of the wood in fifteen minutes," commanded Barry, taking a cup of tea from the moist hand of an orderly behind the trestle-table. "I will meet you there."

"Yessir." Sergeant Cannonroyal saluted again, but made no move to go.

"What is it, Sergeant Cannonroyal?"

Barry drank the tea, and dragged back his gaze from the door of the Club, where Mrs. Lovecome had disappeared, to the Sergeant's face.

"Beg pardon, sir, I doubt if twelve of the men is available, sir."

"What the devil do you mean?"

"Very short of men this afternoon, sir."

"How's that?"

"Fifty of them is in the clink—ahem—Guard-house, sir—after that bit of an argument with the Fifth Irish last night."

"That leaves another fifty. Go and get twelve at once."

"Beg your pardon, sir. There's a lot gone sick."

"I never heard such—who's gone sick?"

"Corporal Brevet, sir. And Mullins, Cornet, Rattle, Biffer, Page, Proot, Cassion and Leary, sir."

"What's the matter with them? Is it an epidemic? Has it been reported?"

"No, sir. Only the staggers, sir. And Miss Nightingale always said——"

"Oh, so Miss Nightingale is Colonel of this Regiment now, is she?"

"Miss Nightingale always said you never know where the staggers may lead to, sir," concluded Sergeant Cannonroyal doggedly. He had been in hospital at Scutari. "Never neglect the staggers was what she always said, sir."

"A pretty pass things have come to, when I cannot get twelve men to go on duty because of Miss Nightingale. By God, that woman has done more harm than an army corps." Barry's voice was very bitter; he had his own reason for feeling furious against women.

Sergeant Cannonroyal's nostrils dilated and his chest swelled, but he said nothing.

"And the other forty, I presume, are lying down with

nervous headaches," continued Barry, relishing, as a young man will, his own sarcasms.

"Twenty is on duty 'ere, sir. Mess-orderlies. Ten's got leave this afternoon, sir."

" *Then—go—and—get—the—other—ten.*"

"Very good, sir."

Sergeant Cannonroyal saluted, and marched away.

Barry took another cup of tea, glanced at the clock above one of the Club doors, and drew up a chair among a group of laughing young ladies and brother officers, who made room for him.

Sergeant Cannonroyal marched across the lawn towards the barracks, with a red wooden face. He was carrying on a furious conversation inside himself.

" 'Oo persuaded me to save twelve pound of my pay? She did. 'Oo saw it got safe 'ome and was waitin' for me when I got 'ere? She did. 'Oo set to and cleaned out the bogs with 'er own 'ands? She did. 'Oo was up to all their tricks and went one better every time? She was. 'Oo just about kept the life goin' in our poor bleedin' bodies and always a kind word and a cool 'and for the roughest poor devil of the lot of us? *She* 'ad. And that stuck-up, red-thatch prize monkey of a shoot-you-in-the-back Irish paddy to call 'er a 'woman'—I'd like to—if 'e gets twelve men for this 'ere business this afternoon, blast my tripes if I ever drinks another pint, so help me Gawd."

Sergeant Cannonroyal here turned aside down a short, wide, paved passage that led between the Club buildings to the parade-ground and the barracks.

"Where's the rest of yer?" he said sharply to a very young private with a pronounced cowlick, who was watering some flowers in a window-box outside the married quarters.

"Down the Pleasure Gardens, mostly," returned the very young private affably.

"Say 'Sergeant' when you speak to me, you griffin, *and*

salute, or I'll give you something so's your wife'll think it's
a stranger in bed with 'er to-night"

A faint cry, and some agitated movements of a rounded
bosom in a print dress just visible behind the new
muslin window curtains, showed that this had gone
home.

"Yes, Sergeant!"

"You on fatigue?" pursued the Sergeant. "Yes, I can
see that," he went on, as the very young private opened
his mouth to reply. "Can't take you orf that. All right.
Shut your trap up again and for Gawd's sake get on
watering yer forget-me-nots," and he marched away,
beckoning as he did so to a drummer-boy who was sitting
in the shade overhauling his drums: every now and again
the soft heavy sound rolled out on the still afternoon air,
while the boy listened with bent head.

"Nip off down the Pleasure Gardens, Taps, and tell any
sodjers you can see to come up here at the double,"
commanded Sergeant Cannonroyal.

The boy put down his sticks, and sped away.

CHAPTER XXI

"AND over there," said Augustine Thwart earnestly,
putting a dirty finger on the paper, "we could 'ave
another croquet 'oop."

"That's right," chorused the group of waiters, nodding.
Some forty of them, with ten or twelve soldiers, whose
uniforms and greater height were conspicuous among the
darkly dressed little waiters, were gathered round Mrs.
Sawyer's shrimpery.

"Lars time I tried to drive in a croquet 'oop I swooned,"

hoarsely said a waiter named Wear. "Dead away.
Weakness."

"Never mind, cock; I'll knock yer croquet 'oop in for
yer," said a big corporal named Target, tapping Wear on
the head with his pipe. "Rely on me."

"It'ull take us a year to save up for it," warned Arthur
Sobber.

The others turned on him.

"Aw, shut yer row. What's the odds, if it's fer the good
o' the Pleasure Gardens?"

They were engaged this afternoon on their favourite
amusement: the planning of improvements in the Pleasure
Gardens. A rough map of the Gardens was spread before
them on a bench and each man had his contribution to
make to the game, though only one scheme in several
hundreds was ever able to be carried out, and of those only
the most pitifully modest.

Even the pleasure of being with their wives and
families was less than the satisfaction of planning a foun-
tain or a cricket ground: the wives were seated this afternoon at some distance away, a collection of drooping mud-
coloured shawls and bonnets from which a droning
murmur arose, and all round them, triumphantly cheerful,
danced the children in their scanty vests. Philly was
sitting up in one of the old trees, while Lieutenant
Toloreaux leant against its trunk and talked to her.

The soldiers were indulgently good-natured to the
waiters' schemes. They were sorry for the poor little
articles: weak, weedy, always being taken in, unable to
protect themselves by the many devices that the Men of
the Regiment had learnt on their various campaigns in
foreign parts, and utterly at the mercy of the swells.

"I see it says 'ere," said another soldier, rustling a copy
of the *Police Gazette*, "as they've got the Bermondsey Beast."

"Wot, 'im as did in them three old gals?" asked a
waiter.

"'Ow did they catch 'im?" asked Target quietly.

"It says 'ere as he was caught red-'anded goin' for a fourth old gal and brought in by a member of the public."

"Funny 'ow 'e always went for old gals."

"You wouldn't think it was funny if you was an old gal. There's five 'undred pounds reward for somebody."

"For The Wolf, you mean," said Target, again quietly, puffing at his pipe. A murmur of amazement went up.

"Do you reely think so, Jack?"

"I knows so. I got a friend in the peelers; 'e tells me a lot. The Wolf's brought in 'alf a dozen murderers this year. The Hampstead 'Orror, that's one; then there was the Leper of Limehouse, and the Dread of Deptford; let's see, that's three, and the Walthamstow Wretch and the Edmonton Excrescence, and now the Bermondsey Beast—that makes six."

"'Ow do they know it's 'im?"

"Same as we do. 'E always leaves a card with 'is name on."

"Must 'ave made a tidy bit out of all them rewards, too," put in a waiter named Bleak.

"And why not?" demanded Rodd, another of the soldiers. "'E earns it, don't 'e? Can't be no joke catchin' murderers red-'anded."

There was a murmur of agreement.

"Then do the slops know 'oo 'e is?"

Target shook his head.

"No more than what we do. The murderers was left tied up outside the peeler-'ouse—just as 'e used to leave the blacks tied up, remember? and the rewards was paid into a bank account 'e gave them the address of, all right and proper."

"I wonder the peelers didn't try and find out 'oo 'e is."

"Why should they? 'E wasn't breakin' the law."

"That wouldn't make no difference to peelers," said Bleak darkly.

"I got a friend in Southend could let us 'ave a sackful of broken shell," interrupted a waiter named Dearth, impatiently; he was eager to get back to the improvement of the Pleasure Gardens. "Just right for puttin' round a new radish bed."

"'Ere," murmured Wear, dabbing at the map.

"Ah, but the reddishes ain't what they used to be. Got no bite to 'em," said a very old waiter. "Nor 'as the crisses. Can't tell you *are* eatin' reddishes or crisses nowadays. Why, when I was a boy they'd burn your tongue 'alf off, the crisses and reddishes would, leave it red and raw so's you couldn't eat the rest o' yer tea."

"Then it's a good thing they ain't like that nowadays," said Mrs. Sawyer, rather sharply. "Puttin' people off their teas. Bad for trade."

"Yes, a new radish bed just 'ere," mused Thwart, "and what say a bed of sweet williams just 'ere? The women likes flowers."

"Pansies," said a very small waiter eagerly. "My sister out at Barnet's got 'em in a bed shaped like a 'eart."

There was a murmur of admiration.

"That's a good idea," said Thwart, and began to draw clumsily with a stub of pencil. "'Eart-shaped bed for pansies *'ere*, radish bed just *'ere*, cress-bed alongside *'ere*, new croquet-hoop——"

Suddenly there was a commotion on the outer edge of the group, and a drummer-boy forced his way between the waiters and up to Corporal Target, whom he breathlessly addressed:

"Corporal Target, Private Footy, all of you, Sergeant Cannonroyal wants you at once."

"Old Shootmequick on the rampage again? Oh, well, come on, mates. No peace for the wicked," and Corporal Target removed his elbows from the bench and stood upright, his comrades doing likewise.

"Wot's up, do yer think?" asked Wear, apprehensively.

All the waiters stared anxiously at Target, who shook his head.

"Nothing, p'raps. Or p'raps—somethink. I dunno no more than you do. All I know is what I told you; the orfficers is very excited about somethink this afternoon. There's a kind of a *feeling* in the air. Like you get before an attack, ain't there, mates?" The soldiers nodded with a deep murmur of agreement and all the waiters looked more miserable, if possible, than ever, while Mrs. Sawyer was heard to mutter that it was a shame to upset them.

"But don't you worrit yourselves," Target went on in a more cheerful tone. "I dare say it ain't nothing. And if it is—we'll stand by you, won't we, mates?" Again the deep murmur, awesome yet comforting. "And whatever you does," advised Target as he and his comrades began to move away, "don't go and do nothing in a *hurry*. It hardly ever works. 'Course, sometimes when there's bleedin' well no other way, you has to charge with the baynit, but most times, if you just takes your time and has a dekko, you can find another way round. So keep yer peckers up, cocks."

"Thanks, Corporal."

"Very kind of you, I'm sure, Mr. Target."

"We'll remember."

"'Ave a dekko and find another way round—he-he! Very good! All right, Corporal."

The waiters all looked much more cheerful as the soldiers moved off. They were all (with the exception of Arthur Sobber) inclined to be optimistic rather than the reverse, and were given to making such heartening prophecies as "O' course he won't take it" and "Naturally, he won't think o' goin' in there" whenever the subject of the Pleasure Gardens came up.

"Poor little runagates," observed Corporal Target, as he and the men made their way back through the little wood. "There's trouble brewin', that's as plain as your face, Footy. And I've got a notion, me lads, as that's what we're a-wanted for this very minute."

As they emerged from the wood they met Sergeant Cannonroyal walking smartly towards them. All halted, and saluted.

"Lieutenant Molloy's orders: you will remain 'ere until 'e arrives, awaiting further orders," snapped the Sergeant.

The men saluted again.

"I take it," continued Sergeant Cannonroyal, standing at attention with his eyes fixed upon the glittering summit of the South Tower, where a cloud lazily floated, "that they will be to proceed to the Pleasure Gardens to serve a proclamation of annexation on the tenants."

Corporal Target and some of the men exchanged glances.

"Privates Footy, Mack, Dawson, Piddler, Warsome and Jones, you will no doubt recall that this afternoon at five o'clock pre-cisely (it now being three minutes to the hour) you was under orders to pipeclay your scran-bags."

"Yessir," answered the men addressed, saluting.

"Corporal Target, you was due at five o'clock, you will recall, at the stab-rags to be measured for a new great-coat."

"Yessir," Corporal Target saluted.

"And you, Privates Mason, Green, Fodder, Tumm, Hughes and Billet, was of course on fatigue on account of your back tags bein' in a disgustin', unworkmanlike and filthy condition calculated to spread alarm and despondency and lower the prestige o' the Regiment."

"Yessir." The six saluted.

"Very well, then. Jump to it," roared Sergeant Cannonroyal; and in another two minutes he stood alone on the edge of the wood beneath the gently rustling green boughs.

In a few minutes, Barry, on Bayard, rode out from under

an archway in the Club, and, on seeing the solitary Sergeant, at once increased the horse's pace to a canter that brought him to his side. The Sergeant saluted.

"What is the meaning of this?" demanded Barry. "Where are your men?"

"Begging your pardon, sir. None available, sir," saluting again. "Privates Footy, Mack, Dawson, Piddler, Warsome and Jones is pipeclayin' their scran-bags— haversacks, sir. Privates Mason, Green, Fodder, Tumm, Hughes and Billet is on fatigues, sir."

"All six? What are the charges?"

"All the same, sir. Back tags in a filthy, disgustin' and unworkmanlike condition calculated to spread alarm and despondency and lower the prestige o' the Regiment, sir."

Barry gritted his teeth. His gaze moved over the barrack-square; in the distance a solitary figure in a scarlet uniform could be seen bending over something that shone, as he rotated it, like a miniature sun.

"Private Tumm, sir. Polishin' the Bucket," said Sergeant Cannonroyal.

The Bucket was the receptacle in which coal was supposed to be carried from the cellars to the Sergeants' Mess. Frequent polishings by men on fatigues, spread over many years, had burnished it to such dazzling lustre that an order was issued that no coal must be put into it for fear of dirtying it. As no second bucket could be issued while the first was still in use, and as the one in use was never used and therefore never wore out, no coal was ever, in theory, carried to the Sergeants' Mess. In practice, a private was told off at the beginning of every winter to carry it across in a sack.

"Where is Corporal Target?" Barry asked; he was very pale, and spoke quietly.

"Corporal Target is at the stab-rag—tailor's, sir. Bein' measured for a new overcoat, sir."

Sergeant Cannonroyal, stiff, correct, standing at attention, looked full at Lieutenant Molloy with round pale blue eyes that positively brimmed with dumb insolence. Sebastopol, snow, lice, frostbite, the merciless Indian sun, the fevered horrors of Scutari, the hard monotonous years of obedience exacted and duty performed in company with comrades as tough and wily and cool as himself, surrounded him like an impregnable fort, and from this he looked sarcastically down—though in bodily fact he looked up—at the officer of six weeks' standing. Fume away, my young cock, thought Sergeant Cannonroyal; grit your snags, clench your fists, fall off that there 'orse, that's worth a better master nor you. Split my tripes if you gets another man but me down there this evenin' to serve that notice on them poor saloop-suckers.

"Saddle your horse," ordered Barry at last: he was pale as death but his voice was completely under control. "Return here in five minutes."

Sergeant Cannonroyal saluted and set off at a trot across the barrack yard towards the stables.

CHAPTER XXII

THE sun was now setting. Golden light filled the sky and poured through the two soaring towers that glittered among long translucent clouds. Some guests were beginning to enter their carriages: an orderly had dared to bolt a prawn sandwich while packing up the dirty plates. But many people still lingered on the lawns, enjoying the cool evening air and wondering why Doctor Pressure had been shut in his study all the afternoon with the blinds down. Some interest, too, was shown in Major Pillichoddie, who had retired under the thick shade of some beech trees at an early stage of the festivities with a whole jug of claret cup and a glass. People kept on coming up and peering at him and trying to make out who on earth it could be in there, sitting with his legs stuck straight out in front of him and a whole jug of cup all to himself, and then exclaiming, "Oh, pray forgive my intrusion!" on noticing the Major's obviously low and melancholy state.

The Colonel had observed this tableau with considerable annoyance. Indeed, there were several large flies in the ointment of his excitement and pleasure: he was at the top of his form in one way; gliding about from one group of officers to another, and dropping a subtle hint here, a sinister warning there, whipping up anticipation about the Pleasure Gardens and voluptuously savouring the tasty mixture of envy, ambition, disapproval, helplessness, toadyism, flattery, hatred, hope, defiance and fear that floated in the air like a smell. (Anyone who has been at a party of professionals who are all in the same line will know it.) But a messenger must be sent to Pillichoddie requesting him not to make a damned fool of himself before Lord Melbourne—and why was Pressure cloistered in his study with all the blinds drawn?

Why, indeed?

.   .   .   .   .

"There you are, Harrovius," said Mrs. Lovecome, strolling into the sanctum. He had shut the windows and drawn down the blinds and got himself right up into a corner where he was pretending to consult a commentary on Pliny. He only mumbled when she entered, and pretended not to see her.

"Page 43, at the bottom," mumbled Doctor Pressure.

Mrs. Lovecome giggled and sat on the table.

"Jenny—Jane!" exclaimed he in an agony, "get down at once—sit properly, in a chair. Suppose the Colonel were to enter?"

"Oh yes, well, perhaps I had better," and she got down and seated herself as he suggested. "Now, Harrovius, we can have our little talk. Goodness, what's all this?" bending over a pile of manuscripts and some drawings that lay on the table.

"It is my life-work: *The History of Weapons Both Civilized and Uncivilized from the Earliest Times to the Present Day*." Doctor Pressure's voice was proud.

"Goodness, what an unpleasant subject!"

"Unpleasant, Jenny—Jane, I should say?"

"Certainly. Also dull, alarming and unnecessary."

"It is well known that the female mind is incapable of finding any subject of interest that does not touch upon infants or dress," said Doctor Pressure bitingly, "and also that females are disconcerted by the spectacle of implements of aggression. But I must say, Jane, that I fail to see why you should describe my *magnum opus* as *unnecessary*."

"Well, Toppendorf has done one."

"Toppendorf? Toppendorf? You mean——" gasped Doctor Pressure hoarsely, reeling against a bookcase.

"Yes. You remember—the one who had the apartment downstairs that you were everlastingly arguing with while the meals got cold."

"He—he went to Leipzig University!"

"Yes, he did, and very kind he was to me, too, when I was so cut up after you'd slung your hook."

"And he—you say he has compiled a History of Weapons?"

"That's what he said the last time I heard from him."

"Both civilized and uncivilized?"

"I don't know for certain, but I expect so. He always was a whole-hogger."

"From the Earliest Times to the Present Day?"

"Sure to be."

For a moment Doctor Pressure remained silent, with

bent head and hands clasped in anguish. Then he looked up proudly and announced:

"Mine cannot fail to be the better work of the two."

Mrs. Lovecome surveyed him, then shook her head.

"If I made half the fuss you do about things I'd have been dead by now. Look here, we haven't got much time; I can't sit here all afternoon with the blinds down; it looks so funny. When are we going to be married?"

Doctor Pressure at once became extremely agitated and retreated behind a bust of Cicero.

"Now, Jenny, Jane, that is, we must come to a final decision here and now. We—er—I have no intention—that is—we cannot be married. I will not deny that I retain a certain—ah—well, I cannot call it esteem—perhaps—ah—*softness* would be a better word—for you——"

"Much better," said Mrs. Lovecome, who was not paying close attention to him but gazing round the room. "Good Lord, who on earth is that?" pointing with her parasol at a portrait over the fireplace.

Doctor Pressure drew himself up.

"A Miss Ida Mould," he said reprovingly. "A good, pure, devoted Christian worker."

"Poor thing," said Mrs. Lovecome compassionately. "Why have you got her up there, Harrovius?"

"It was necessary to provide Beatrice with a portrait that could be—referred to as her mother," muttered Doctor Pressure, going red.

"And so you got her, with hardly any hair and that chest, to give you her portrait?"

"Well—ah——"

"You *are* unkind, Harrovius!" cried Mrs. Lovecome indignantly, "I expect she thought you were in love with her."

"At one time I did seem to detect—but doubtless I was mistaken."

"Doubtless you weren't—waving your beard at her and saying bits of Greek and Latin to the poor thing. And where is she now?"

"She—ah—went to Siam as a missionary, I understand."

"I do think you're mean, really I do. I can't imagine why I'm going to marry you—except that you *are* Beatrice's father and you *do* look rather sweet when you're asleep and it *was* fun in the attic in Heidelberg, wasn't it? Do you remember making garlic salad?"

Doctor Pressure stonily shook his head.

"And how you always tied my scarf round my head before I went out to work every morning, and held Beatrice up at the window to wave good-bye to me?"

"You were incapable of securely adjusting your own headgear, otherwise I should not have done so," retorted Doctor Pressure stiffly.

"And how good Beatrice always was, playing in her chair with her blue beads while you studied? I've got those blue bleads still."

"I do not wish to hear about them!" roared Doctor Pressure, and at that moment the door slowly opened and a voice said softly:

"Ah, a thousand pardons, Doctor Pressure. I did not know that you were—engaged."

"May I present Colonel Delawarre—Mrs. Lovecome," muttered Doctor Pressure, and the Colonel bowed languidly over Mrs. Lovecome's pale lavender glove.

"And are you, dear Doctor Pressure, also thinking of entering the married state?" said the Colonel in a terrifying and serpent-like whisper, drawing his head back and half shutting his almond eyes as he looked balefully at Doctor Pressure.

(Mrs. Lovecome had withdrawn to a side table and was studying some prints of Rome.)

"Merciful Heavens, no, Colonel," stammered Doctor

Pressure, thrown into new transports of alarm. "Nothing is further from my thoughts, I assure you."

His discomfort was increased by the fact that in the act of drawing the blinds across the windows he had observed Beatrice actually strolling with that whippersnapper, Venner, towards the conservatory; but so terrified was he of encountering Mrs. Lovecome that he had been afraid to venture out and summon his daughter to his side.

"I think Lord Melbourne is looking for you, Colonel Delawarre," observed Mrs. Lovecome quietly; she had drawn one of the blinds a little aside and was gazing out into the splendid afternoon.

"Ah; thank you," said the Colonel vaguely, and bowed to her and went out.

"Well, I must be going, too; some tea would be most grateful," said Mrs. Lovecome cheerfully, adjusting her bracelets. "Are you not going to have some, Harrovius?" for the Doctor had sat down by his manuscript and was gazing despondently at it. "Oh, are you worrying about Toppendorf, dear? I *am* sorry; it *is* a shame; but that is the worst of these popular subjects. When we are married I will help you to think of another subject, something really unpopular."

"We—are—not—going—to—be—married, Jane."

"Oh, yes we are, and soon; in about three months; and Beatrice can marry that *excellent* Captain Venner at the same time; she would make a lovely winter bride in white velvet and red roses, and I shall wear amber; Worth would do it, if we let him know at once."

Doctor Pressure groaned and buried his face in his hands.

While adjusting the details of gloves and necklace preparatory to setting out, Mrs. Lovecome had still been looking leisurely about, and now noticed the little drawer, especially painted with sorrowful black paint.

"Whatever's in there!" she cried, and swooping across

the room she opened it, revealing the little stool embroidered in red silk with a glass of wine.

For a minute there was silence, while she stood looking down at it. Then she said in a wonderfully soft voice:

"Oh, Harrovius. You kept it. I *do* think that was sweet of you. You must love me a little, you know, or you wouldn't have done that."

"I do not love you, Jenny—I mean Jane," roared Doctor Pressure, refusing to remove his hands from his face, but Mrs. Lovecome, dropping a light kiss upon his grey curls, strode out into the sunlight.

Doctor Pressure remained at his desk, turning over the pages of *The History of Weapons Both Civilized and Uncivilized from the Earliest Times to the Present Day*, and occasionally drawing a great sigh. The blinds remained down, and as no one brought him any tea and he was too much on his dig. to go out and find some, he sat there a prey to the gloomiest forebodings about wedding-cake and went without.

CHAPTER XXIII

DOWN in the Pleasure Gardens, the waiters had forgotten *their* forebodings as they drank a final cup of saloop before returning to their duties.

Mrs. Sawyer was one of the few shrimpery-keepers who still brewed saloop, an old-fashioned beverage decocted from the root of the red-handed orchis. It comforted the waiters' stomachs because it was greasy and warm. In less than an hour they must return to their duties, but meanwhile they sipped the tipple and relished, as much as their cramped faculties would permit, the coolness and hush that fell with the drawing-on of evening.

Philly had come down from her tree and was now wandering along the edge of the wood with Lieutenant Toloreaux's arm about her waist and her black straw hat swinging in one hand.

"Never fear, love," the young man was saying. "No doubt there is some good reason for the delay."

"But if the money should never come!"

"Why, then, my darling girl, we must be married in secret."

"Oh, Gerard!"

"Does the thought distress you?"

"Oh, no—how could I be distressed at the idea of me being—married to you? It's only——"

"That you wanted a wedding-dress?"

"Yes, Gerard—and—and little Emma Sobber and Harriet Thwart to be my bridesmaids."

"You shall have them, love, never fear. I will write to my uncle's men of business again this evening."

"I promised Emma and Harriet," murmured Philly, gazing away towards the waiters' wives and children. Some of the larger children, who were past the vest-and-hopping stage, were playing with rags in a corner under the leadership of two little girls with dirty yellow hair.

"If only You-Know-Who don't shoot you when he finds out you want to be married to me," sighed Philly next. "He takes on alarming about people getting married, Ma always says."

"He cannot object when I am no longer a member of the Regiment."

"That's why he shot Pa, for marrying Ma. Well, we *think* so. 'Course, we don't really know. He happened to run into Pa one day when it was Pa's afternoon off; Pa was very happy that day 'cos we was all a-going on the river, and You-Know-Who whipped out his pistol and shot him. No reason given."

Ticky tenderly pressed her plump arm. She was about

to speak again, when he quickly drew her into the shelter of some bushes, and at that moment Lieutenant Molloy, followed by Sergeant Cannonroyal, rode out of the trees.

Barry's face was expressionless and pale; the Sergeant's looked as if it were made of wood. Followed by the alarmed and fascinated gaze of the lovers, they rode down the course of the stream until they drew rein in front of the shrimpery.

"Ah!" said Ticky. He had seen the roll of parchment with its purple ribbons and copper seal carried by Sergeant Cannonroyal.

A hush fell on the group of waiters as the shadows of the two horsemen, long in the evening sunlight, fell across them. Silence, too, seemed suddenly to come over the Pleasure Gardens. The children stopped their games and ran to their mothers' skirts; Mrs. Sawyer, who was at that moment lifting a kettle of freshly boiled shrimps off the fire, set it down again and collapsed upon a bench, gazing fearfully up at Barry's stony face.

Slowly his gaze moved from one man to another, as if seeking their leader, and at last his cold blue eyes became fixed upon the largest of the waiters, who happened to be Augustine Thwart. Barry motioned to Sergeant Cannonroyal, who, sitting very upright, unrolled the parchment with a crackling noise that sounded loud in the stillness and began in a loud impersonal voice to read, as if to Augustine Thwart:

Whereas it has come under the observation of the authorities that a new drill-ground is necessary for the maintenance of the First Bloods Regiment and whereas it has come under the observation of the said authorities that the piece of waste-ground three hundred yards square situated between the place of public refreshment known as The Bugle Blast and the wood immediately beneath the North Tower is at present lying uncultivated and unoccupied except by divers tenants who hold squatter's presumption thereon, it has been decided to turn the said piece of ground (hereinafter known as Drill Ground Number Eight) into a drill ground. The authorities will take possession of Drill Ground Number Eight on October 31st 18——, being one month from this present date.

Signed: EUSTACE DELAWARRE,
Colonel.

Sergeant Cannonroyal then dismounted, stalked across to the shrimpery between the lines of silent white-faced waiters, and affixed the proclamation to the cottage door. Then he remounted, Barry gave a last slow haughty glance over the shrinking crowd, and the two soldiers rode away.

The purple ribbons fluttered in the breeze. Augustine Thwart put out a hand that trembled uncontrollably as if to touch the proclamation, but let it fall to his side again. No one spoke. The only sound was the bubbling of the shrimp kettle.

The silence was broken by Mrs. Sawyer. She rose from the bench where she had collapsed upon seeing Barry, and came forward just as Arthur Sobber opened his mouth to speak. But Mrs. Sawyer got in first.

"Arthur Sobber, if you say '*It's no use, mates, we got the Monkey's Allowance again,*' I shall *scream*," said Mrs. Sawyer vehemently. "Now, all of you—Sobber, Gast, Wear, Dearth, Down—have another cup of saloop all round; it'll warm you up and you've got another twenty minutes before you need go back on duty. Come along—here, Gast, drink up"—as she spoke the good soul was ladling the brew into the cups and handing it round—"now cheer up, my lads, the sodjers is on our side; Corporal Target said so."

"Ay, that's true," murmured one or two, beginning to feel the reviving power of the decoction.

"And—and there's a munf before it—happens," went on Mrs. Sawyer, pressing shrimps and watercress into their nerveless hands and speaking she knew not what in her attempts to lighten their looks. "A lot can happen in a munf."

"Ay, that's true," they muttered dully, eating and drinking.

"And, besides——" suddenly said a new voice; a young, strong, kind voice, as the head and shoulders of Lieutenant Toloreaux appeared behind Wear, and he clapped both hands upon the little man and gently swayed him backwards and forwards. "What's the row about? You've got your Charter!"

A roar of relief burst forth. Silk hats, shrimps and empty mugs were flung in the air. Wear seized Gast and whirled him round. Thwart tried to stand on his head. Mrs. Sawyer clasped her hands together and raised her eyes to heaven in thankfulness.

"Three cheers for the Charter!"

"Good old General Ramm!"

"We'll show You-Know-Who, you just wait!"

"That'll learn 'im!"

"Freedom, Peace and Plenty, don't it say?"

"Thassit. I remember my Dad used to tell of it. '*To 'ave and to 'old in'*—somethink—'*an*' *Freedom, Peace an' Plenty, for as long as*——' somethink. I carn't rightly remember."

"Thassit. Freedom, Peace and Plenty."

"All we got to do now is to show it to 'im."

"'E won't 'alf be wild," said someone timorously.

The others turned on him.

"Let 'im! 'E carn't do nothing. It's the Charter, ain't it?"

"Our Charter."

"We've always 'ad it. Ever since there *was* waiters."

"Three blinkin' cheers for the Charter!"

Again everyone threw their silk hats and mugs into the air. When they came down again there was a lull, and Arthur Sobber suddenly asked:

"By the way, where is it?"

CHAPTER XXIV

NO one answered him for a moment. Then Augustine Thwart said heartily:

"Why, it's—it's—ain't it up the Tower, along of the daguerreotypes?"

Some shook their heads; others nodded.

"Yes, that's where it is!" said Gast. "Come to think of it, I'm sure it's up there. If I shut my eyes I can see it."

"I can't," said Wear.

"'Aven't you got it, Dearth?"

"Me? What should I 'ave it for? Catch me carryin' a blinkin' charter round the Rookery with the young gents' bath-waters."

"Testetti? You was climbin' up the doorposts repaintin' your precious motter yesterday. Ain't it stuck up over the door?"

"No, no, no, no, no, no, no." Testetti shook his curly black head. "I nev-a have-a seen it. I tink it a story you make-a up."

"Like your ruddy imperence, then."

"All charters of Freedom, Peace and Plenty are makeups. I tink-a so."

"Oh, well, you're a foreigner. That's different. Come on, mates, this is gettin' serious. Don't none of you know vere it is? Scragg! You keeps the money for Improvements to the Pleasure Gardens. Ain't it in that there tin box?"

Scragg, a melancholy little man, shook his head.

"Nuffin' in there but farthings, cocks."

(The waiters were each paid three farthings a week as pin-money. Roof, food and clothing were provided by the Regiment.)

Augustine Thwart wiped his forehead. All the rest were beginning to look serious and pale once more. Mrs.

Sawyer was gazing anxiously from one worried face to the other, but thinking what silly dolts men were, never able to lay their hands on a thing they wanted.

"P'raps some of the womenfolk have got it?" suggested Ticky; then, drawing out his gold hunter, he exclaimed in dismay: "Oh, by George, I shall be late for Mess!" and with a hasty kiss on Philly's cheek, hurried away. He called over his shoulder as he went:

"Take heart, my good friends, it is bound to turn up."

But the waiters' faces were getting paler and paler and slowly the light of hope died in their eyes. The ribbons of the parchment still fluttered gaily in the twilight breeze, now borrowing a regal glow from the purpling sky while the copper seals caught the last gleam of sunset.

"Well, you must all start huntin' for it this very night, that's all," said Mrs. Sawyer briskly. "(Philly, don't stand gawping there after Lieutenant Toloreaux, ducks, give me a hand with these benches.) Now, what's the Charter look like?"

"Werry large and 'andsome."

"Small but rich-like, I remember my Dad saying."

"A great big piece of parchment with—with red seals."

"Blue," corrected a voice. "Lions and crowns on it."

"All over gold braid." "Lovely black writing," said several voices at once.

"Then it ought to be easy to recognize," said Mrs. Sawyer with sarcasm. "I suppose it ain't got a couple of bells and a birdcage on it, by any chance? There, it's a shame to tease you, poor souls," observing their dejected looks. "Me and Philly'll start at once, this very evening, asking your wives and children. Cheer up. Don't despair, dears. God will help you. We'll all pray in earnest, and put our trust in Him that careth for the sparrows, and I *know* it'll be found."

"I 'ope so," muttered Arthur Sobber, but he shook his head.

Suddenly the fire-alarm sounded; it was the signal for the waiters to return to work, but they had been deceived by it so many times that none of them hurried much. They shuffled off, making sketchy gestures of farewell to Mrs. Sawyer and Philly, who stood watching them go. Their dark figures looked small and forlorn under the darkening heavens.

"Poor creatures," muttered Mrs. Sawyer, turning away to continue with packing up for the night. "And them wives o' theirs isn't much use to 'em, I'm sure. Do you know, Philly, what that Mrs. Scragg says to me yesterday? I was saying as how I'll lay the waiters' sleeping quarters could do with a broom round 'em, and she says, 'What's a broom, Mrs. Sawyer?' *What's a broom*! Gave me quite a turn. And her with six children!"

"Fancy. Mum, could you spare me to-morrow afternoon to go off down the market and buy a new ribbon for me bonnet? Green."

"I s'pose so. The other ain't wore out yet, is it?"

"And the fourpence, will you spare me, Mum?"

"I s'pose so."

The young moon was rising over the little wood and the trees kept up a sweet romantic sighing. Mrs. Sawyer had now retreated into the cottage and was sitting by a brazier and gazing thoughtfully into its flames, while Philly was lighting a broken brass lamp. Slowly the warm light shone over the green mossy walls, the two beds spread with straw, the loaf on the table and the kettle singing quietly above the red coals.

"'Urry up and get the tea made, ducks," said Mrs. Sawyer absently. "I can just about do with a cup."

Outside the autumn night was starry and chill. Dead leaves blew across the deserted Pleasure Gardens. The windows of the Club blazed with light like a fairy palace.

"Ah, I hope them poor souls finds their Charter," said Mrs. Sawyer, rousing herself to begin on her tea. "What they'll do—what we'll all do—if they don't, I don't know."

   .   .   .   .   .

So began the great search for the Charter.

"Good Ged, what's this?" exclaimed Major Baird, distastefully examining a dirty scrap of paper found upon his pillow while his batman was assisting him to dress for dinner in the Mess. It was a week later. He screwed his glass into his eye and read:

O sir if you are The Wolf please elp us to find our Charter. O sir even if you don't want us to ave the pleasure gardens justice is justice and if you are The Wolf you will want us to and will help us we have looked everywhere.

Signed

and there followed in a remarkable variety of hands the names of Scragg, Dearth, Wear, Sobber and some hundred more.

The waiters had searched for the Charter without ceasing for four days and nights, working in shifts of twenty, each shift's work being done by the others while it was absent on the search. They had turned the benches in the shrimpery upside down and tapped them for hollow places; they had taken the daguerreotypes down and examined the backs, pulled the thatch off Mrs. Sawyer's roof and put it back, turned their straw beds inside out, questioned all the oldest waiters among them to try and find some legend or tradition about where the Charter had always been kept, brought upon themselves the mirthful scorn of the young gentlemen at the Military School by timidly questioning them, crept into the chapel at midnight and searched in its chests, cupboards and drawers, tested the Improvements To The Pleasure Gardens box for secret compartments, and alarmed the wives and children by prolonged and exhaustive questioning: and these were only a few of the things they had done; there was not a place accessible to them that they had not turned inside

out and upwise down—in vain: and at last they were
forced to the despairing conclusion that the document was
concealed among the archives of the Regiment in the
Colonel's own quarters.

All but Scant. He was the only one who clung obstin-
ately to the tradition that the Charter had always been
kept by the waiters, not by the officers. He said his old
Mum always used to say so, adding that if she had been
still happily with them she would very soon have found it,
which called forth the retort from Wear that no doubt
those who hide can find.

Tempers, in fact, were getting short and strained as the
first week drew to an end and the Charter had not been
found. A shrill hysterical note came into the waiters'
voices: one of them name Bone broke a plate belonging to
a valuable regimental dinner-service and was shot in the
leg by Barry: this was the first waiter he had winged and
the officers stood him a dinner in honour of the occasion.

In their trouble the waiters had even fallen in with the
suggestion, put forward by Dearth, that they should appeal
to The Wolf. If anyone could help them, he could. They
knew that he was supposed to be one of the officers, and
had therefore left a copy of their appeal in the apartments
of all of them, even the Colonel himself, though everyone
except Dearth had blenched at this thought.

"'Ow *could* it be 'im?" argued Wear. "Is it likely '*e'd*
steal chops for the likes of us?"

"Cut us up into 'em, more like," put in Down.

"If You-know-'Oo is The Wolf, I'll never believe me
own eyes or ears again. I shall just go mad, that's all, and
you'll 'ave me on your 'ands," said Gast solemnly.

"Not for long we won't," Dearth assured him. "No,
mates. Stranger things 'ave 'appened in this world than
You-Know-'Oo being The Wolf. My Pa was a gipsy, and
I know. So we'll leave a message for 'im same as all the
others."

Major Baird now put the scrap of paper in a note-case that had been embroidered for him by fair hands.

"Devilish amusing. Take it along and show the Mess," said Major Baird to himself.

His batman, who happened to be Private Brevet, had, read the note before his master came in and was awed at the waiters' daring. "Them articles must be fair desperate," he thought.

The soldiers, to a man, sympathized with the waiters, and the officers were beginning to realize it. In fact, there was a growing feeling that the officer who led the Men down to take possession of the Pleasure Gardens on the appointed day might have to face an unprecedented situation. The word "mutiny" had never, needless to say, been so much as breathed in the long and glorious history of the First Bloods, but—there certainly was an unfamiliar and ominous smell in the air, and experienced officers, such as Major Pillichoddie, were very uneasy.

Major Baird got briskly into a private tram and wrapped himself tightly in his winter greatcoat, collared and lined with astrakhan. The journey up to the North Tower was even colder now that autumn had set in.

He felt pleasantly fatigued. Like the Colonel, he was continually testing the men for endurance and courage and trying, without much result, to work up a bloodthirsty spirit among them. He was for ever creeping up behind Private Brevet or Bloggs and violently punching them in the small of the back or putting the half-nelson on them and then complaining that they did not defend themselves with sufficient ferocity. He also carried a little bottle of cat's blood and water and was everlastingly sprinkling the men with it at bayonet drill and ordering them to pretend that it was the blood of Rooshians or Prooshians or whoever happened to be the enemy of the moment. Private Pringle said that the cat must have died of laughing at Major Baird, and that was the only result he and his blood-sprinkling produced, the men being by this time expert at dodging these belligerent cascades.

The driver of the tram happened to be Emmanuel Licker, the father of George. Licker was the only one of the waiters who had a good opinion of himself: he always seemed to have a warm suit and enough to eat and it was whispered that he earned pocket-money by spying on his comrades. He had never been popular and was even less so now that George, under the Colonel's patronage, had become a bugler.

He obsequiously unwrapped Major Baird when they reached their destination and begged for the stump of his cigar, which the Major threw him.

"Thank you, Major, a thousand times, I'm sure, Major," said Emmanuel Licker, bowing. "Going to be a fine night, Major," for the harvest moon was rising above the roofs of London and the trees of the Park far below.

The Major signed to him to wait with the tram, and passed on into the Mess.

All the officers were standing about the great log fire, comparing their notes amid much laughter from those who constituted the Colonel's party. Ticky smiled, but without much amusement; Major Milde and Captain Gabriel were pensive and silent. Major Pillichoddie was shaking his head.

"Faugh! the effrontery of it is almost inconceivable!" exclaimed the Colonel at last, glancing again at his note with a contemptuous smile. "I am flattered, indeed, that they should imagine I might be The Wolf. True, it would not be out of keeping with my character if I were, eh, Molloy?"

"No, indeed, sir."

"Daring, secrecy, an almost foolhardy courage—I think I fill such a bill, do I not?"

"In every respect, sir."

"True, I am a man of feeling, curse it. That is my

weakness. Feeling." He let his eyelids droop over his almond eyes. "And I feel for these creatures—I—feel— very—much. They call on *justice*, I observe," shaking the note slightly as he held it and looking round from under lowered lids at the firelit circle of silent men, "and I am disposed to see that they have it. Their Charter, I gather, is missing. That is unfortunate. We will help them to look for it. No one can say that justice has been denied to them, when I, the power which is going to dispossess them, I myself join in the search for the document which, if found, can confute *me*."

There was a murmur of assent.

"Good!" cried the Colonel, clapping Major Milde on the back and causing him partly to swallow the stump of the cigar he was just finishing. "We will go up to the North Tower later on and make a *thorough* search. And now—to supper!"

Laughing and talking, the party moved over to the table. The Colonel, lingering a little behind the others, beckoned to one of the orderlies.

"Sir?" said the man, springing forward and saluting.

"Tell them to have Wolfram and Adelbert, Cedric and Hereward in readiness below the South Tower in two hours from now," commanded the Colonel in a low tone.

"Very good, sir." The man saluted and made off.

They were the names of the Colonel's bloodhounds.

CHAPTER XXV

THAT evening, Doctor Pressure and Beatrice were sitting in the drawing-room after dinner.

The greens and crimsons of the room were dimmed by

the twilight, for only one candle burned above the piano, and through the window, where the curtains were not yet drawn, streamed in the light of the moon. Beatrice, in a white gown with a pale blue cashmere shawl about her shoulders, was singing, while her father, sitting upright as a poker in the most uncomfortable chair in the room—and there was a good choice—was apparently listening.

1

Be silent, my fevered soul,
As the dew of evening falls,
And the light of day fast fades away
And the bell o'er the meadow calls.

2

The waves break slow on the shore,
The shadows creep from the west,
The young birds sleep in the forest deep,
O heart! sleep now in my breast.

3

Though darkness cover the land
Heaven's light shall fill mine eyes
When the longed-for day for which I pray
Shall break in the eastern skies.

4

Patience, my restless heart,
The hush of evening falls,
Light dies in the west, and from my breast,
And the bell o'er the meadow calls.

The song ended with a solemn chord.

"Very suitable," observed Doctor Pressure, rousing himself with a start. "What is its title?"

" 'The Bell o'er the Meadow Calls,' Papa."

"Indeed. I have heard it before, have I not?"

"Oh yes, Papa."

"Very suitable," muttered Doctor Pressure again, and returned to his thoughts.

"Would you care for me to sing again, Papa?"

"No, I thank you."

"Do you mind if I continue with my work, then, Papa?"

"What is its nature?"

"Netting, Papa. I am netting a purse."

"Oh yes, pray continue."

"Shall I ring for the lamps, Papa?"

"No. That is—no. Not just yet."

Beatrice was silent. Without the lamps she could not see to work comfortably, but she did not like to ask for them to be brought in after her father's last remark: she got up from the piano, crossed to a chair, and sat down and once more was silent.

Presently Doctor Pressure, who was now, to her distress, sitting with his head in his hands, gave a groan.

"Papa! Will you not have this chair? It is more comfortable."

"No, I thank you."

"Would you like me to fan you? or to ring for some toast and water?"

"No, I thank you."

"Would you like to look over to-day's note for *The History of Weapons*?"

This time the only answer was a louder groan.

Beatrice's anxiety was considerable, but for the first time in her eighteen years she had affairs of her own to reflect upon; moving, hopeful affairs, and whereas only a few weeks ago she would have been unable to settle to her work while her father was so plainly disturbed, she now got up and went over to the window; she was eager to finish her purse.

Doctor Pressure felt, rather than saw, her white dress glide past his chair.

"Pray sit still, Beatrice," he commanded from behind his fingers, "you are very ill at ease this evening, suggesting all kinds of changes of posture and occupation. I wish to be quiet."

"I am sorry, Papa, if I vex you; I only desired to see if the moonlight were bright enough to work by."

"Ring for the lamps, then, if you must."

"Oh no, Papa; it is so bright, I can see quite well," and in a minute the needles were flashing to and fro as she sat by the open window with the half-completed purse of lilac silk.

Presently, after stealing one or two glances at her father, who still sat in the same position, she began softly, yet resolutely:

"Papa?"

"Beatrice, I have said that I wish to be *quiet*."

"Yes, Papa, but——"

"And I shall be obliged if you will be silent."

"Yes, Papa. I only wished that to-night you would speak to me a little of Mamma."

After a pause Doctor Pressure said hoarsely:

"And why should you have such a wish on this evening in particular?"

Colour came unseen into Beatrice's face, and she looked down at her slippers.

"Oh—I do not know, exactly why, Papa: the night is so beautiful, and I have been thinking of her so much to-day, wondering what she was like——"

"Does not a portrait hang in my study?"

"Oh yes, Papa, but I have always wondered if—if it is really like her," said Beatrice in a low tone, and glanced swiftly at her own moonlit reflection, white dress and pale-blue shawl and glossy braided hair, that was reflected in a mirror on the opposite wall.

"It is an excellent likeness," said Doctor Pressure loudly.

Beatrice sighed, as if she had hoped for another answer.

"There are so *many* things I would like to have told her," she said, as if to herself. "Not things of great importance, perhaps——"

"I am always in my study, as you know, from ten o'clock each morning until twelve noon," said Doctor Pressure; he had removed his hands from his face and sat upright and seemed to have recovered some of his usual manner, "and though I cannot truthfully say that I shall be *glad* to receive female confidences of a doubtless trivial and foolish nature, I consider it my duty to do so (in your case) and I am willing to do so. I will even go so far as to say that their triviality need not deter you from imparting them to me. If you are perplexed about any matter, however small—let us say, as to what family the Water Lobelia is attached, or whether the Wall Hawkweed has a terminal or a lateral corymb—you have only to impart it to me."

"Thank you, Papa."

"I will do my best to dispose of it and I have little doubt but that I shall succeed."

"You are so kind, Papa."

"I hope that I am conscious of our duties here below, Beatrice, as I hope that you are."

"Yes, Papa."

There followed a little silence, in which Doctor Pressure might have been observed to stifle a deep breath, as of relief in having avoided a dangerous topic of conversation. Then he concealed a yawn, and after glancing somewhat vacantly about the room, dim red and green in the moonlight, brought his gaze back to the ethereal figure of his daughter.

"And what," he inquired, "are you engaged upon at this moment? Some charitable work for the Parsees or the Pawnees?"

"It is a purse, Papa."

"Surely our good friends the Pawnees have but scant use for purses?" and here Doctor Pressure permitted himself a sonorous, if brief, laugh at the weakness of the female intellect and the misapplication of female effort.

"Oh no, Papa, it is not for the Pawnees, it is for Mrs. Lovecome," answered Beatrice, looking tranquilly across at him.

Doctor Pressure flew up out of his chair; then slowly subsided again, never removing his gaze from his daughter's face.

"Mrs.——?" stammered Doctor Pressure.

"Yes, Papa. The singer, Madame Jeanne. She has been so kind to me. Yesterday I went to see her school for young ladies in Belgrave Square."

"You—you—went——"

"Yes, Papa." Beatrice looked a little surprised and alarmed. "Lady Venner was going there, and I happened to be calling on her, and she took me in her carriage. Lieutenant Molloy was there, too, calling upon Mrs. Lovecome. I hope you are not vexed that I went?"

"No matter—no matter——" muttered Doctor Pressure. "And this—establishment—what is it like?"

"Oh, it was so pleasant!" broke forth Beatrice, dropping her work and clasping her hands. "The girls wear such a pretty uniform, grey batiste with white soutache braid, and coloured ribbons on their hair, and they learn to cook and mend and make clothes and play picquet and read aloud and dance and cultivate vegetables, and bath and dress babies, and at the same time they all read History and Philosophy! Is not that strange, Papa?"

Doctor Pressure was just opening his lips with the word "Bedlam!" to usher in a tremendous speech, followed by the strict forbidding of Beatrice ever to visit the establishment again, when a confused sound of voices and the deep baying of dogs sent him hurrying to the window, where Beatrice, half-concealed by the curtain, was already gazing out.

By the brilliant glare of the moon, they saw a torchlight procession making its way across the great square towards the North Tower. It was headed by a tall figure in a purple cape lined with copper satin that gleamed as its wearer's vigorous motion set the folds moving; the unusual grace of movement betrayed the Colonel. He carried a torch, whose smoky brilliance wonderfully stained the moonlit air; and the six or seven gentlemen who followed (Beatrice sadly identified the sweeping golden beard of Captain Gabriel among them) also carried torches. Four very large bloodhounds accompanied the procession; these, while undoubtedly adding to the picturesqueness of the proceedings, did raise a doubt in the mind as to what the deuce the officers and gentlemen were up to.

They raised one in the mind of Doctor Pressure, who put his hands behind his back and tapped one upon the other, lowered his beard onto his chest, and said, "Tt-tt-tt." In a moment he muttered, "Man is born free but is everywhere in chains," and went on to quote a passage from John Stuart Mill in praise of Liberty. "Military discipline, of course," muttered Doctor Pressure, gazing, and tapping his hand, and shaking his head. "Most necessary, no doubt. Nevertheless—Freedom, Peace and Plenty. Liberty, Equality, Fraternity. By George, should one go after one's brothers with bloodhounds for defending their rights? Still"—he turned away from the window—"no doubt military discipline. . . . It would be wisest, I think, to draw the curtains."

He did so, and rang the bell for the lamps.

CHAPTER XXVI

A S soon as the procession crowded into the North
Tower through the heavy door that was half off its
hinges, all the torches went out, and there went up a
general chorus of, "Phew!"

"Bats!" exclaimed Major Baird, as a large one flapped
past him out into the moonlight.

"Cats," muttered Cussett, wrinkling his nose.

"Is that what it is?" inquired the Colonel.

His upbringing in a castle and subsequent career had
been so luxurious that he had never previously encountered
this odour.

"Beg pardon, sir, them articles keeps a lot of moggies
in 'ere." The voice of one of the privates who was
holding the dog Hereward came resignedly out of the
darkness.

"Where the deuce is the tramway?" demanded the
Colonel.

"Beggin' your pardon, sir, no tramway 'ere, sir. Them
articles goes up the staircase," said Private Fodder.

"Relight the torches," commanded the Colonel
impatiently.

"Very good, sir. 'Ere, catch 'old of Fido, will yer,"
whispered Private Fodder, passing Hereward's leash to
the other soldier.

In a moment the rosy light flared up again. It shone
on excited pale faces, giant cobwebs and slumbering bats,
glittering uniforms, the heavy ears and mournful eyes of
the dogs, and the mouldering wooden rails and treads of
an ancient staircase winding up and away into a vast spiral
of shadow. The torchlight could not reach up there. It
soared into the gloom and was lost.

"Who will lead the way?" demanded the Colonel,
stooping to lift gently aside a ginger cat lying in dirty

straw with some wriggling kittens; he had nearly trodden on them.

Major Milde, and Ticky, who had managed to get to the back of the procession, were exchanging agonized glances.

"If he sees what's up there, those poor devils will grill," whispered Ticky. Major Milde nodded.

"We must keep him in conversation, that is the only hope," he answered. "Do you offer to lead the way. Think of some excuse."

Ticky pushed his way to the front of the crowd and respectfully saluted.

"I think I could find the way up, sir."

"How do you come to know it?" demanded the Colonel sharply.

"My aunt's spaniel, sir, ran up the staircase after a cat last Founder's Day, and I was compelled, to relieve my aunt's distress, to pursue and capture it."

"Very well. Lead on."

In a few moments, with Ticky and the Colonel at its head, the procession was moving slowly upwards. The torchlight flickered on piles of mouldering sacks and rubbish, and occasionally there was the white gleam of a skeleton, whether that of a very large cat or a very small waiter, it was not possible to discern.

Suddenly the Colonel's voice rolled forth musically.

"Disgraceful! The place is a veritable lazar-house! How many years, Molloy, since it has seen soap and water?"

"Forty at least, sir, I should judge."

"And yet the proportions are noble! The staircase is well designed! It should have a crimson repp carpet, pots filled with the commoner plants in the windows, clean cotton draperies. Everything appropriately humble, yet spotless. That is how, in my mind's eye, I see it. Curse!" and the Colonel recovered his balance as he tripped.

"It would be as well, sir, if I may be permitted to make the suggestion, to keep the eyes fixed upon the staircase," interposed Ticky respectfully. He had been peering ahead into the gloom, and observed that they were approaching the first danger-point.

"I am doing so," snapped the Colonel.

"Do you not agree with me, Pillichoddie," he went on, "that creatures who keep their living quarters in such a condition do not deserve a Charter—if, indeed, ha! ha! they ever possessed one?"

Major Pillichoddie gave a gruff mutter in reply in which the only intelligible words were "Bonaparte" and "Christian duty."

"Carefully here, sir!" cried Ticky's warning voice, "some of the stairs are broken quite away."

It was the custom of the waiters to gather at this spot and stand admiring the large fresco, painted by some unknown waiter-hand long since sunk in oblivion, which represented the Colonel as Satan in command of a group of fiends, bearing the lineaments of Major Baird, Major Pillichoddie and the rest of the officers. The Colonel had nothing on and the details of his person were limned with loving care. Underneath the cartoon and all about it were numberless rhymes and smaller drawings made by less gifted waiters, including a feeble sketch of the shooting of Mr. Sawyer signed: A. Sobber. *Sculpt. et Pinx.*

Just as the tail of the procession was passing the masterpiece, one of the gentlemen—Captain Gabriel, in fact—happened to glance up and was confronted by the full-length figure of the Colonel drawn upon the wall. Captain Gabriel, appalled, started back with a loud cry of "Good Gwacious!" but at that moment his torch fell from his hand—or struck against something, he never knew which—and vanished into the dark gulf. Presently, very far below, he saw as he peered over the railing a blaze of sparks flare up and heard a faint agonized "mi-aow!"

"What is the matter there?" cried the Colonel impatiently, hearing the shouts and commotion.

"Nothing alarming, sir—Captain Venner has dropped his torch."

"Pray be more careful, Venner," snarled the Colonel, "these torches cost eightpence halfpenny the piece," and on Gabriel's saluting and answering, "Vewy good, sir," the procession continued. I must have been the victim of a howwible hallucination, thought Gabriel. What a stwange thing, though.

Major Milde breathed again. There was another picture to be passed, but this was so much higher up that he hoped the Colonel might have tired of his caprice and turned to go down again before they came to it: he hoped it very heartily indeed.

And the Colonel was already showing signs of weariness.

"How the deuce much further is it?" he demanded, pausing at the next spiral of the staircase and turning fretfully to confront his companions.

"We are about half-way, sir, I judge it," answered Major Milde at once.

"How the devil do you know?"

"I was with Lieutenant Toloreaux, sir, on the occasion of which he spoke just now."

"Oh, you were, were you? Well, well, let us go on. The stench of this place is sickening," and the Colonel, his usual panther glide now changed by weariness to a sort of stomp, doggedly set out again.

Suddenly there was a cry. Someone pointed, shouting, at a pale face glimmering above them in the shadows. A shot rang out, and it vanished.

"Missed him, by George!" exclaimed Dannit. Smoke was issuing slowly from his pistol.

Wear, who had been sent out on reconnaissance by the terrified waiters in their quarters at the summit, flitted up the stairs again in the gloom. His heart was thundering and cold sweat was on his hands.

"They're all there!" he cried, bursting through the ragged sackcloth curtains and facing his trembling comrades. "Oh, Gawd, what *shall* we do?"

"It's no use, mates, we got——"

But a voice interrupted Arthur Sobber before he could finish the despairing sentence. It came from a figure standing in the gloom with a military cloak drawn across its face so as to obscure every feature save the eyes.

"Destroy the stairs. And may God defend the right!" it commanded in low but ringing tones. And before the waiters could move, the figure darted back into the shadows and was gone.

"It's The Wolf, God bless 'im!" cried Dearth.

"Come on, mates! Jump to it! We'll beat 'em yet!"

He snatched up an iron stave and rushed to the head of the staircase, followed by Scant, Gast, Wear and the rest.

All fell to with a will, and no one took any notice of Arthur Sobber as he languidly attacked the bannisters with an old fork and kept on asking how they was going to get down theirselves if they broke up the blinkin' stairs? Other people might be willing to stay up here and starve to death, but he, Arthur Sobber, liked a relish with his tea.

"Hark!" commanded the Colonel, standing still and holding up his hand for silence.

All stood motionless, listening. The distant noise of chopping and hammering and the crack of breaking wood could be heard, but even as they listened, the sound ceased and all was still.

"Well, let us go on, they are up to some mischief, no doubt," said the Colonel. He spoke without enthusiasm and yawned as he did so. Ticky and Major Milde exchanged hopeful glances. The torches were burning low and through the windows poured the ghastly light of the setting moon.

As they all stood there uncertainly, and the Colonel stifled a second yawn, Major Pillichoddie turned upon his heel and began deliberately to descend the staircase.

"Ha, Pillichoddie—what, weary of the chase so soon?" called the Colonel.

"My dear Eustace, I have to be on parade at ten o'clock," testily replied the Major, feeling his way down into the dimness. Then his voice was suddenly cut off as he turned the corner. The others stared doubtfully at the Colonel.

"Ah, pah, the night is yet young!" cried he, springing upright, "Come, gentlemen, follow me!"

The privates hauled up the dogs, who had flopped on the stairs and gone to sleep, and, exchanging hopeless glances, resumed the ascent.

"Because 'e was up till three o'clock don't mean *we* can 'ave dirty bo'sun's whistles to-morrow on parade, *oh*, no," observed Private Cornet in a gloomy whisper.

"You're about right, mate."

The ascent continued. There were now hardly any whole stairs, and dark caverns gaped between them where the grey form of a rat occasionally glimmered. The dogs pulled at their leashes and bayed after them and the waiters, huddled at the head of the stairs, turned sick with terror.

Suddenly the stairs ended. There was nothing but a great black hole with shreds of splintered wood hanging down into it.

"Look out, sir!" shouted Cussett.

The Colonel had just saved himself, with the help of Lieutenant Molloy and Ensign Cussett, from falling headlong into the abyss.

"Good Gad!"

"What an escape!"

"Do you sit down and rest a moment, sir, I entreat you!"

The Colonel, thus implored, seated himself upon a sound stair and consented to partake from Major Milde's brandy flask. While drinking, he glanced upwards. The staircase continued nine feet overhead.

"That's done yer," grimly whispered Scant, hauling up the last coils of a thin greasy rope down which the waiters were accustomed to slide all the way to the ground when they were in a hurry. "And you don't go using our hand-railway, neither." The waiters were gathered just beyond the next turn of the staircase, peering down into the gloom. They could see the flicker of the torchlight and hear the haughty tones of the officers' voices.

Ticky was relieved to observe that they had had the sense to break up the stairs immediately below the second fresco, which represented the Colonel burning in Hell while the waiters held a ball and supper in his private apartments. Care had been taken to keep Mrs. Sawyer from hearing in detail about this picture, for in it she was represented as a sort of triumphant saint, crowned with watercress and carrying a harp, and sitting on the Colonel's bed. It was dimly felt that her principles, which were respected rather than comprehended, would prevent her from relishing her transfiguration.

"Shall I send Private Warsome down for a ladder, sir?" inquired Cussett.

The Colonel hesitated, and Private Warsome, rigid with horror, held his breath.

"No, I think not," said the Colonel at last with a pleasant laugh. "The truth is, gentlemen, I fear that if we linger here the mephitic airs may endanger your healths."

There was a murmur of gratitude, carefully not mingled with relief.

"So we will make our way downwards," concluded the

Colonel, standing up. "Tell the men to light fresh torches, Major Baird."

This was done; and in a moment there came to the eager ears of the listening waiters the welcome sounds of retreat. Voices grew fainter, the terrifying scrabble of the hounds' nails upon the stairs died away, and the last flicker of torchlight faded. At last the waiters were alone, crouching in cramped positions in the chill of the dawn whose light was slowly growing upon their white faces.

"They've gone," at last sighed Bone.

"I tink-a perhaps one of dem hide-a down dere, and wait-a for us?" suggested Testetti, shivering miserably and remembering the sunlight blazing down upon the blue sea of Portfino Bay.

"It 'ud be just like 'em," agreed Thwart. "Go on, Wear, you're messenger-lad to-night, you just nip down and see."

But Wear had fallen asleep with his face on a dirty sack.

"I'll go," said Bleak, who, being of a foolishly hopeful nature, felt certain that the officers had all gone.

In a moment he was back, waving a sheet of paper above his head. The others crowded round to see.

"Stuck in the stairs with a pin," explained Bleak.

By the wan light they read:

"Heaven knows, my dear fellows, I would help you if I could, but I am as ignorant of your Charter's whereabouts as are your goodselves. But take heart! Much can happen in three weeks!" It was signed "The Wolf."

There was a heavy silence, broken at last by Augustine Thwart.

"Much'll 'ave to, unless we're goin' to get the Monkey's Allowance again (if *Mister* Sobber will excuse the liberty?). Well, I'm goin' to bed. I got to be on duty in three hours."

Dejectedly, with drooping heads, they climbed the ladders to their bunks.

.　　　.　　　.　　　.

The officers reached the ground once more without mishap; but just as they were leaving the Tower the Colonel observed that the ginger cat was looking at them very balefully from among its wriggling kittens, and licking some singed fur.

"What ails you, puss?" he gently inquired, bending to stroke its head with his long fingers. The cat gave an angry miaow and glanced in the direction of a shattered and extinguished torch that lay at some distance away, and the Colonel also observed signs of the kittens and their bed having been newly dragged into their present position.

"Captain Venner!" he snapped, standing upright.

"Sir?"

"I am as surprised as I am indignant that you should vent your ill-temper upon a harmless animal engaged in its maternal duties. Consider yourself under arrest, and report yourself to Major Pillichoddie to-morrow morning."

"Vewy good, sir," answered Gabriel stiffly, saluting.

"There, puss," said the Colonel, stooping once more to stroke the cat.

The cat sulkily shut its eyes, and the officers and their Colonel stepped out into the still air of morning.

CHAPTER XXVII

"PAPA," inquired Beatrice, standing at the door of Doctor Pressure's bedchamber one morning a week later, "do you feel very unwell?"

"Not 'very' unwell, Beatrice," sharply corrected the Doctor, who was lying back upon the pillows in frilled nightshirt and a nightcap. "A slight recurring faintness, feverish tremblings, confused noises in the ears, an increased pace of the heart and sharp pangs in the—sharp pangs, in short, compel me to forgo my usual activities for to-day, at least. But it were an exaggeration to say that I am 'very unwell.'"

"I am so relieved, dear Papa."

"I shall remain quietly here," went on Doctor Pressure, "and meditate. I have given every instruction, of course, about my lectures for to-day; so that there is no need for me to be disturbed. At noon I will partake of a light refection—let us say, some toast and water and barley gruel—such a refection would in no way, of course, be regarded as a substitute for luncheon."

"I will tell Bodder, Papa."

"Do so. And now hand me *Bore Upon the Jutes*—no, *no*, that is a Circassian grammar. *Bore Upon the Jutes* is what I require—*no*—now you have given me *Notes on Early Saxon Religious Musical Pipes*—I asked for *BORE—BORE UPON THE JUTES*."

"I think you are lying upon it, Papa; there is a book just under your pillow."

"Oh—ah? is there?—yes, exactly so: I thank you. Well, no doubt you have your morning duties to perform. You may look in upon me again immediately before luncheon."

"Yes, Papa. I hope that you will then be feeling better, Papa."

Doctor Pressure made a vague and lofty movement of the hand without looking up from *Bore*, and Beatrice glided away so quickly that it might have been suspected that she did not wish to be questioned about the nature of her morning duties. She went straight upstairs to her room and took out all her bonnets and put them in a row and sat down and stared at them.

It was now about ten o'clock. The Doctor's apartments were quiet, for Bodder, his manservant, was busy in the pantry, the maids were employed in the kitchen and

Sour was in the sewing-room, engaged in ironing Beatrice's petticoats. Fine rain was falling steadily through the trees and the leaves came down in golden showers at the light touch of the drops and lay on the grass, so green beneath the grey sky.

Doctor Pressure held *Bore* upside down and pretended to read, with no peaceful expression upon his countenance. A guilty conscience and apprehensions about the future were responsible for his present symptoms.

The rain fell; a clock chimed the half-hour; and a distant bugle-call came from the barracks. Then a light step sounded outside the Doctor's study, and a lady dressed in a dark violet travelling-cloak and veil appeared, and saw with surprise that one of the French windows had been left unlatched. It was Mrs. Lovecome.

She stepped into the room and stook shaking the rain-drops from her umbrella and moving her little wet boots to and fro upon the Doctor's carpet.

My pet must be upstairs, she thought, and was going towards the bell-rope to summon a servant to announce her, when a sound at the window made her start and turn round. A young man stood there, with the silver rain upon his red uncovered curls, gazing at her.

"Lieutenant Molloy—how pleasant!" exclaimed Mrs Lovecome, thinking, *Now this is going to be really awkward, I can feel it in my bones*. "How are you after all this long time?"

"We met only yesterday evening at your house. Does it seem like a long time to you?" he said eagerly, coming into the room.

"So we did, and you went home in a temper."

"I was a brute," he said passionately, drawing nearer to her and never taking his gaze from her face.

"Oh, come now!"

"Yes, I was. A mad, ungrateful, unfeeling brute!" still advancing as he spoke.

"You are too severe upon yourself," said Mrs. Love-come, cheerfully, but beginning to move away from him.

"I have not slept all night for remorse at my boorishness."

"Indeed?" Mrs. Lovecome murmured. She was now driven into a corner and in another moment would bump into that bust of Cicero mentioned upon a previous occasion.

"You are running away from me!" exclaimed Barry, in pain and delight. He tried to take her hands, which she immediately popped behind her back. "Mrs. Lovecome —Jeanne—my lovely flower—are you afraid of me?"

"Of course not, but I hate struggling with people and I'm afraid of knocking this beastly bust over," she retorted frankly. "Oh, don't *loom* at me!" pushing past him and striding into the middle of the room and sitting down. In her agitation she chose the table (her seat in many such encounters) for it gave her confidence to swing her pretty feet.

Barry came slowly towards her again, but this time the look on his face made her unable for the moment to say a word. Unresisting, she let him gently take her hand, and gaze at it with an expression almost awed.

"Loveliest of creatures——" he began. And then he said again, "Loveliest——" but could not go on, and turned his head aside that she might not see his tears.

She suffered her hand to remain in his, and was silent. Oh, how I wish *they wouldn't*, she was thinking. Here am I, a perfectly good woman—well, *wanting* to be perfectly good, at least—and only longing to take my rightful place in society as my darling's mother, and this is the way they *will* go on.

"It is not my fault," she said at last.

"The sea might say as much when it drowns men."

"They need not go to sea."

"How can they help themselves, when it draws them so?"

"I do assure you, my dear boy, that I have never tried to draw *anybody*," said Mrs. Lovecome very earnestly. "All I ask is a quiet life with a little gaiety every now and then, preferably of an innocent nature. It distresses me more than I can say to see you in this state, and I would do anything within reason——"

"I do not want anything within reason."

"Then I am afraid I can do nothing to help you."

There was silence for a moment.

In the pause, Doctor Pressure was agitatedly fastening about his person the cords of a voluminous plaid dressing-gown and shuffling his feet into bedroom slippers. He had heard the voices coming from his study and was convinced that Toppendorf had bribed someone to break in and steal the manuscript of *The History of Weapons Both Ancient and Modern from the Earliest Times to the Present Day*, and was preparing to rush out and deal with the intruder.

Barry passed his hand across his eyes.

"I insulted you at the garden party," he said in a low tone. "Can you ever forgive me? I invited you to dine with me alone! I must have been blind not to see at once that you are as good as you are beautiful."

It's a blessing you don't know how nearly I said "Yes," thought Mrs. Lovecome, looking up at him out of her limpid brown eyes and feeling pleased at this tribute. She preferred to be told that she was good rather than that she was beautiful, for it was not her beauty that needed moral support.

"When I saw you walking across the grounds to-day I followed you," he went on, "determined to ask you to marry me. Will you? Oh, Jeanne, my angel, my flower, I implore you to marry me!"

And down went Lieutenant Molloy gracefully upon one knee, with his hand upon his heart.

In spite of her years and her devotion to Doctor Pressure
and her daughter, Mrs. Lovecome could not meet the
beautiful pleading eyes and hear the young voice without
some emotion. She afterwards recalled that the phrase
What a lark it would be! drifted across her mind—to be
instantly dismissed.

She answered (and even as she spoke the door of the
study was stealthily opened by Doctor Pressure, and at the
same instant the tall form of Colonel Delawarre stepped
across the window)—

"You do me a great honour, Lieutenant Molloy.
Nevertheless, I can only advise you to bestow your devotion upon some young girl who shall be worthy of it——"

"Never!"

"For I am already betrothed."

"His name?" gasped Barry.

"Doctor Harrovius Pressure," proclaimed Mrs. Lovecome very clearly indeed.

There was immediately a loud cry from the prospective
bridegroom, who dropped the poker he was clutching and
staggered into an arm-chair.

"Why, Harrovius, dear!" exclaimed Mrs. Lovecome.

"So, Lieutenant Molloy," said the Colonel in a terrible
sneering whisper, "*this* is the explanation of your failure
to appear at the butts half an hour ago! You have crept
away to keep a tryst!"

"Good morning, Colonel Delawarre," said Mrs.
Lovecome, fanning Doctor Pressure with her cloak and
thinking what a damned nuisance men were, "why, we
are really a little party, are we not? Lieutenant Molloy
and I met quite by chance——"

The Colonel coldly saluted.

"I am relieved to hear it, madam."

"Now, Colonel Delawarre, I am afraid that you do not
believe me."

"Ladies are never disbelieved, madam." The Colonel

did not put the faintest emphasis upon the first word; nevertheless Mrs. Lovecome thought, *That's one in the eye for you, Jenny.*

Here Doctor Pressure, maddened by the raindrops that were being flicked into his face, sat up and furiously pushed the travelling-cloak away, exclaiming, "Enough, enough, I thank you, I am perfectly restored."

"So glad, dear," said Mrs. Lovecome.

Then there was silence for a moment while they all stood staring awkwardly at one another. Rage, desire and despair were struggling in Barry's heart, and ambition was there as well. He had no wish, now that Mrs. Lovecome was apparently lost to him, to lose his chance of a military career also. He made an effort, and said hoarsely, but calmly:

"No meeting with Mrs. Lovecome could be described so ungratefully as an accident, sir; rather, it must be regarded a direct gift from the gods. But in this case it is true that my encounter with her was unforeseen."

The Colonel did not answer, but looked slowly from one to the other, pulling at his moustache, and ignoring Doctor Pressure, in whom symptoms of distress were once more apparent. There were heavings of the dressing-gown and the words "Bodder—toast and water—assistance——" could be faintly heard.

"Bodder, dear? That is your man, is it not? Do you desire him to assist you to your bedchamber? Lieutenant Molloy—will you be so kind?——" and Mrs. Lovecome indicated the bell-rope while she bent solicitously over her betrothed. Barry gave the bell a savage tug.

"I am distressed to see you so indisposed, Doctor Pressure," said the Colonel in a very disagreeable voice, "but no doubt your great happiness is responsible for your agitation. We are to congratulate you, are we not? and when is the *wedding* to be?"

Doctor Pressure made no reply save to utter a fresh

moan, with closed eyes, for Bodder and the toast and water, but Mrs. Lovecome looked limpidly at the Colonel.

"In December." Her tone was dignified yet modest. "May we hope that you will honour us with your presence, Colonel Delawarre, and you too, Lieutenant Molloy?"

"The Regiment will probably have left for Afghanistan, madam, by December," rejoined the Colonel coldly, "but if the pressure of our military duties permits and if the occasion does not escape our recollection, we will endeavour to be present. Come, Lieutenant Molloy, we are already forty-five minutes late at the butts."

The two officers saluted, Barry without looking at Mrs. Lovecome, and stepped out through the windows into the rain.

"There! Now we can be comfortable, Harrovius dear," and Mrs. Lovecome patted his shoulder. "What I really came to see you about was this. Have——"

"Bodder—Bodder!"

"You rang, sir," said Bodder's alarmed voice at the door.

"Yes, Bodder." Mrs. Lovecome turned smilingly to him. "Please bring negus and biscuits, and have the fire lit; the morning is chilly and this damp air is not good for your master, and Bodder, pray shut the windows."

"Very good—sir—madam, that is," and Bodder, with a respectful yet admiring glance, withdrew. Doctor Pressure, observing this capitulation with one eye open, was too dismayed to utter a word. But at last he sat up, pulling his dressing-gown tighter about himself, and said faintly:

"It is highly improper, Jane, that you should be here—alone, at this hour, in boots!"

Mrs. Lovecome made no answer save to put her finger on her lips and smilingly shake her head, for Bodder had returned with the biscuits and negus and one of the maids, whom he instructed in a low voice to put a match to the fire while he himself shut the windows. Doctor Pressure permitted himself to be supported to the fire by Mrs. Lovecome and Bodder and sank into a comfortable chair and shut his eyes. When he opened them again, some time later, he found Mrs. Lovecome sitting opposite to him with her petticoats drawn up to reveal her ravishing ankles, and a glass of negus in one hand. She was gazing pensively into the flames, and when Doctor Pressure uttered a hoarse cry of horror at the sight of the ankles, she turned slowly towards him as though coming out of a daydream.

"Harrovius, what I was going to say was," she began, "if you are not going to do any more work on *The History of Weapons Both Ancient and Modern from the Earliest Times to the Present Day*, may I have it? The girls are very short of curl-papers."

A very long silence followed this speech. Doctor Pressure sat there, just looking at her. He opened his mouth once or twice. He flung out his hands. He clenched them above his head. He even shook them in the air. But not a word did he utter, and Mrs. Lovecome continued to gaze thoughtfully into the flames and every now and then to sip her negus. Outside the rain fell steadily and the golden leaves floated down, and within the firelight danced over the walls of the room, made dusky by the shades of a winter morning.

. "What, dear?" said Mrs. Lovecome absently at last, turning from the fire. She thought that Doctor Pressure had said something.

"I only observed, Jane," said Doctor Pressure hoarsely, "that you have triumphed."

"Oh, I *am* so glad, dear!" cried Mrs. Lovecome, sitting upright with shining eyes.

"I can resist no longer," continued poor Doctor Pressure, "a woman who can propose that the manuscript of my *magnum opus* should be used for curl-papers. It argues (to quote Molassus the Elder) '*a degree of determination hovering vulture-like above a fathomless abyss of frivolity,*' against which I am powerless to struggle. Let us be married, Jane, when you will."

"In December!" cried Mrs. Lovecome.

"I care not when it be."

"And I may write to Worth to-night?"

"Now, at this instant, if you choose."

"And I may tell Beatrice that I am——"

"By all means. Tell the Colonel, tell Lady Venner, tell the very waiters."

"Lady Venner already knows, dear. Oh! how happy I am!" and she flung both arms round his neck and kissed him.

"Yes; very well; that will do, Jane," said Doctor Pressure, after a little while. "Er—have you still the blue necklace of which you once spoke to me?"

"Oh, yes, indeed, Harrovius!"

"I should like—that is, I suppose it is my duty to see it at some time."

"You shall indeed, dear Harrovius."

"Despite some typical female faults, Beatrice is a good girl."

"Beatrice is a *pet*."

And gradually they went on to speak of Beatrice and her future happiness; and presently when she came downstairs to look in upon her papa before luncheon, she was amazed to find them sitting together hand in hand in the firelight, and to see Mrs. Lovecome rise and come towards her, saying:

"My darling, is that you? I have something to tell you, Beatrice."

CHAPTER XXVIII

THE announcement of Doctor Pressure's betrothal and forthcoming nuptials did not make such a sensation as it would have done in more tranquil times, because there was now only a week to go before the Pleasure Gardens were taken over, and everybody was in such a stew—pleasurable or otherwise—about the missing Charter. Comment was therefore left chiefly to the young gentlemen of the Military School, who excelled themselves, and could be seen at almost any hour of the day dodging behind bushes wearing bridal veils made of unmentionable paper or coyly putting curtain rings upon one another's fingers and then kicking one another.

The announcement was followed by another a few days later: Miss Beatrice Pressure was betrothed to Captain Gabriel Venner and her marriage would take place at the same time as that of her father. The females—the soldiers' and waiters' wives and Mrs. Sawyer—found this particularly touching; but poor Philly, amid her interest and sympathy, could not help feeling how different was Beatrice's lot from her own! Ticky had received no reply to his last letter written to the lawyers who were his uncle's executors, and was in low spirits as a consequence. He also dreaded to see the waiters deprived of their poor heritage, but could do little, beyond sometimes joining in the search for the Charter, to help them.

The Colonel was so furious when he heard of Gabriel's betrothal that he refused to allow Doctor Pressure to put up a notice about the weddings upon any of the regimental notice-boards: he put a private on guard before each one, with orders to tear the notice down as soon as it was put up by Bodder, who had set out hopefully with a whole sheaf of notices. When Bodder reported for the fifteenth time that the notice had been pulled down, Doctor Pressure was reduced to having it put upon the Military School notice-board, all among the announcements about forthcoming cricket matches, and there was much comment from the young gentlemen on the doves and orangeblossom and lace that adorned it.

The ink should be silver, the paper heavenly blue, to write of the happiness of Beatrice and Captain Gabriel. For the first time in her life, Beatrice spoke and moved and looked as a girl should, while his brother officers again heard the sound they had missed for years, Gabriel's leonine laughter.

The nobility and gravity of her betrothed's nature did much to calm Beatrice's spirit, which was troubled by the secret it now held, and as much agitated as charmed by her newly found mother. While rejoicing deeply to learn that she had a mother living, she could not but deplore the circumstances in which she found her; betrayed, abandoned, forced to toil with unwomanly energy for her daily bread, and perfectly cheerful. It was most strange indeed; almost shocking; and Beatrice at length decided that Mrs. Lovecome was one of those unfortunate beings who lack the solemn and necessary sense of sin. Sometimes she prayed earnestly that her mother might acquire it, but when she was with her she loved her so deeply that she often forgot Mrs. Lovecome was a lost soul. The latter, meanwhile, continued to buy a good many pairs of bronze boots and petticoats made of Valenciennes lace and send frequent telegrams to Worth. Doctor Pressure was embarked on a new work, a *Commentary Upon the Text of Molassus the Younger's Notes Upon Molassus the Elder*, and declined to take any notice of the preparations for the wedding beyond suffering Bodder to send his best trousers to be cleaned.

From the North Tower, glittering dimly beneath its covering of ancient soot, sadness and terror mingled with defiance seemed to breathe. Dull lights burned all night behind its grimy upper windows and the shadows of the waiters, searching, searching, ever wearily searching, were thrown grotesquely upon the damp walls.

Within, all was in chaos. The straw beds streamed down from the bunks and the sackcloth coverings were thrust anyhow between the rungs of the ladders. The daguerreotypes were all tossed in one confused heap, together with broken combs and tin basins with holes in and a few cracked plates and chipped mugs from which the waiters ate and drank.

There was always a waiter or two lying in the bunks, sleeping exhaustedly after a night spent in searching, and every now and then one of them would spring up with a shout and begin to fumble dazedly with the walls—searching for the Charter even in sleep. They were now as thin as skeletons, red-eyed from sleeplessness, hoarse from asking eagerly, " 'Ave yer got it, mate?" and "P'raps it's in——" any place, however fantastic and inaccessible, that had not yet been ransacked.

There had been another note from The Wolf, found under a cover in the middle of a chicken-liver omelet that was on its way to Major Pillichoddie. It said:

"Heaven help you, my dear fellows; alas! I have done my best, but cannot."

This had cast the waiters into the deepest abyss of despair that they had yet fathomed: if *The Wolf* had given up hope, who were *they* to cherish it?

Only Dearth and Scant continued to hope; Scant on the unsubstantial grounds that his old mother had always said the waiters had the Charter, and Dearth on the equally flimsy—and rather irritating—ground that his Pa had been a gipsy, and therefore he knew. On being peevishly pressed to explain *what*, he said vaguely that he had a feeling that all would come right. Wear said sombrely that it was a good thing somebody 'ad, and Arthur Sobber got as far as prophesying that once again it would prove to be a case of getting the Monk—when somebody stifled him in a mattress and he was heard no more that night.

And so the days drew on towards the thirty-first of October.

     .   .   .   .   .

It dawned calm and chill. Mist wreathed the two mighty towers and their summits were hidden. Drops fell heavily from the trees and the air smelled of rain. The muffled notes of a bugle blew from far away, sounding the Reveille, and the waiters, the womenfolk, the officers, and the Men stirred in their sleep, rolled over and awoke, and remembered what day it was.

Half an hour later the Men were pipeclaying their bo'sun's whistles in the barracks; deftly, but in a sullen silence. They resented the orders that they would have to carry out that afternoon, and Sergeant Cannonroyal was devoutly hoping that the waiters would not put up any resistance; if they did, anything might happen. He, too, hated the duty that lay before him, and showed it by getting furious with everyone on very little provocation.

In his luxurious chamber the Colonel was sipping his morning tea and ruffling the sheets of the newly warmed *Times*. But he was not reading; he was gazing dreamily at the dull morning sky showing between the crimson window draperies and smiling to himself. To-day—to-day the Pleasure Gardens would be his!

The other officers were performing their toilets in varying states of irritation, distress or pleasurable anticipation. Cussett had dropped in to discuss his morning chop with Dannit and they were seated before a roaring fire, eating and laughing and laying wagers on the nature of the afternoon's proceedings. Barry was moodily staring at his reflection in the glass while Badd adjusted his epaulettes and calculating what benefit he could derive

from the Colonel's triumph; while three doors away
Major Pillichoddie had been reduced by his perplexity
and distress to saying his prayers. Major Baird, with his
mouth full of rather underdone steak, was sitting with a
book propped up in front of him called *Aggravation As An
Aid to Warfare*; he was just mastering the chapter on
supplying the troops with socks too small and boots too
large. Ticky was having a last-minute look for the
Charter in his collar-box; his pink face was quite pale
with distress and he was wishing with all his heart that it
were evening time and the miserable affair over. Even
as he sent collars flying all over the bed in his rummagings,
his batman came in with a letter upon a salver.

"The morning's post, sir."

Ticky glanced at it, recognized it as being from his
late uncle's lawyers, and snatched the letter from the
tray.

Dear Sir,

In reply to your communications of the 18th July, 18th
August, 28th August, 30th August, 4th September, 10th
September, 20th September, 29th September, 4th October,
12th October, 20th October and 27th October, we beg to
assure you that yes, the legacy left in trust for you by your late
Uncle, Richard Toloreaux, Esq., is "perfectly safe"; that no
"misfortune has overtaken" it, and that furthermore it awaits
you at the above address whenever you should care to call and
collect it.

Mr. Preep, Snr : desires me to add that he has, in conjunction
with Mr. William Preep, Mr. Leonard Preep, and Messrs.
Francis, George and Albert Preep, undertaken the care and
management of incalculable sums of money for the last forty-
five years on behalf of most of the nobility and aristocracy of
England. In these circumstances Mr. Preep resents the nature
and frequency of your inquiries as to the "safety" of your own
legacy. He has, however, taken into consideration his long
acquaintanceship with the late Mr. Richard Toloreaux, your
uncle, and desires me to state that the Firm is willing to

continue the management of your affairs, trifling though they be.

>   I am,
>   Yours faithfully,
>   Preep, Preep and Preep,
>   Preep, Preep and Preep.

"Eureka!" cried Ticky, flinging the letter into the air, "Hurrah! Mine at last! A fig for old Preep, confound him! I'll go and get the blunt this very morning!"

"Beg pardon, sir; you're on duty at ten o'clock, sir," interposed his batman, who had been watching with delighted sympathy.

"Confound it, so I am. Well, to-morrow, then. Gad, I'm as happy as a bird! Green, did you ever own a kitten or a cuckoo clock? Put on my sash, I mustn't be late to-day. I've come into a fortune."

"I'm right glad to hear it, sir."

"Thank you, my good fellow; there—that will do. Gad!" he ended, in a quieter tone, "to see her dear face when I tell her the news!"

And he hurried out.

Although there had been no official notice given as to the hour at which the annexation would take place, it was generally known that it was to be at half-past three that afternoon, and everybody was determined to be there or bust. Doctor Pressure was working away like mad at *Molassus the Younger*, in order to have the afternoon at leisure, and upstairs Sour was thumping steadily on the ironing-board with the same object in view. Beatrice was at her desk, working at her household accounts and being given no help by her mother, who had set affairs in train for the day at her school and come over to peep into Doctor Pressure's cupboards and stay on for luncheon and the afternoon's ceremony. Much I care what happens to the old Pleasure Gardens, thought Mrs. Lovecome, but I ought to be there when anything's going on, just to get everybody used to seeing me. Good gracious, what a charming fruit dish, put away and never used. Oh well, another few weeks and I'll have *that* out on the table again; and she carefully blew the dust off it.

The young gentlemen of the Military Preparatory School had been given a half-holiday for the occasion, and The Bugle Blast was shut up for the afternoon (much to the fury of the young gentlemen, who had planned to spend their holiday therein) and Bella had invited Father Doogood to act as her escort to the ceremony, calling on their way for her brother, Badd, and some of the other batmen. The Colonel had subtly encouraged everyone to be present, for he wanted the humiliation of the waiters, the final defeat of their rebellious spirit, to be witnessed by as large a crowd as possible, and so he had affably given his assent whenever anyone had asked for permission to attend.

CHAPTER XXIX

THE dreary day drew on. The sun was hidden behind cold clouds and a bitter wind blew. In the North Tower all was despair. Some of the waiters were feverishly making themselves weapons from jagged beer bottles and old clothes props and lengths of rope and half-bricks. Augustine Thwart had got so interested in constructing a large catapult on wheels that he had quite forgotten what was going to happen and snapped absently at his fellow-waiters when they came up to ask him for orders. They were hastily trying to form themselves into an army, to resist to the death, and Agneo Testetti, who had marched with Garibaldi's Thousand and was therefore assumed to have a practical knowledge of military procedure, had been implored to drill them. It was in vain that he told them that his task had been to spur on The Thousand by blowing the piccolo in the band; they insisted on lining up in front of him with their clothes props at the slope and their despairing eyes fixed with dog-like confidence upon his face, waiting for him to make them into soldiers.

Others were prising stones out of the wall in a half-crazy last-minute search for the Charter; yet others were drawing up a round-robin addressed to The Wolf, and a small, calm party of five was steadily perfecting itself in the accurate throwing of a pickle-jar packed with flints, and had been doing so since five o'clock that morning. These waiters intended, if the worst happened, to do the Colonel in.

Whenever a waiter glanced hopelessly out of the window to take a last look at the beloved Pleasure Gardens, he saw a motionless patch of mud colour grouped upon it, surrounded by a number of tiny red objects that moved. It was the waiters' wives, praying, while all round them hopped the children, now wearing their scanty winter shawls.

Two o'clock struck from the clock on the barracks and sounded on the bugles.

"Now, Philly, my girl," commanded Mrs. Sawyer, pushing aside the plate from which she had been eating tripe and onions, "give me a hand with these potatoes and chestnuts."

"Lor', Ma, you surely won't trouble baking chestnuts to-day?"

"I surely will, my girl. Why, to-day's just the time everybody will want something—all worked up and feverish as they'll be. And fill the great kettle and open the new box of tea. Ah! it's strange to think this may be the last time you and me'll ever make tea on this here brazzier."

"*May* be the last time, Ma? You don't think there's any hopes of it being found, then, do you?"

"We need never despair, Philly, while we are in His hands who careth for the sparrows. Trust and pray, that's my motto. And if everything goes wrong—well, still trust and pray."

"Yes, Ma. How many potatoes shall I put out?"

"All the sackful, ducks. *And* the sack of nuts. Ah me! Twenty years I've been here, and it's passed like a dream in the night. Twenty years!"

"Where'll we go to-night, Ma, if we're turned out?"

"Miss Badd at The Bugle Blast says we can sleep under the bar just for to-night, lovey, and by to-morrow Lieutenant Toloreaux's promised to have somewhere for us to go."

"*Miss Badd*, indeed! She gives me the sick."

"She might be worse, Philly, and if we're going to be beggars we can't be choosers. Hullo, who's this coming along?"

A figure in a purple cloak was running out of the wood towards the cottage, shouting something and waving a white paper. For a moment Mrs. Sawyer and Philly had a wild hope that the Charter had been found—then the runner reached them, and Ticky's arms were round Philly and his kisses were pressed rapturously upon her fresh young face.

"Best and dearest! We have come into our fortune!"

"Oh, Gerard!"

"'Tis all written here!" and he flourished the paper above his head. "I have but to go to the lawyer's office, and it is ours."

"Oh, Gerard!" said Philly again, quite pale with joy. She clasped her hands and looked solemnly at him, while Mrs. Sawyer shut her eyes and said a short heartfelt prayer of thankfulness. Then she opened them and set about filling the kettle and splitting the chestnuts, the while running over in her memory a pattern for a baby's shawl.

"And now we can be married the moment I have purchased my discharge, my dearest girl, and set about buying the little house in Devonshire——"

"With sunflowers in the garden."

"And the cuckoo clock in the nursery."

"And the kitten?"

"And the kitten, of course."

"Oh, we shall be so happy!" and they fell into one another's arms.

"There, there," said Mrs. Sawyer in a moment or two, when she deemed that it was time to recall them to this world of discipline and duty, "that will do now. Lieutenant Toloreaux, do you lift the great kettle on to the brazzier, and Philly, set these nuts to roast with the potatoes. Mercy me, how I wish it was all over and we had seen the worst. Lawks a *mercy*, Mr. Sobber, how you frightened me!"

Arthur Sobber, wrapped from head to foot in sacking with a hood that almost hid his face, had glided noiselessly into the cottage.

"Arternoon, Mrs. Sawyer. Arternoon, sir. Arternoon, miss," he muttered.

"What on earth are you meant to be—the Monkey's Allowance?" demanded Mrs. Sawyer, walking all round him and staring.

"Some of us thought it was appropriate. Mourning, and all that. There's six of us got up like this."

"What's all the others doing?"

"They're going to be an army, I think. Agneo Testetti's drilling them. But me and Down and Bone and a few others, we thought this was more appropriate. Do you like it, Mrs. Sawyer?" turning himself anxiously about and gazing at her.

Mrs. Sawyer banged a saucepan down very hard and

said nothing for a minute. Then she requested Arthur
Sobber to step outside, as the cottage was already full of
people and there was a lot to do this afternoon. He obeyed,
and was presently joined by other figures similarly clad,
who stood in mournful attitudes with bent heads, gazing
at the ground.

Ticky seated himself upon the bench beside Philly, with
one arm round her, and gazed at the great kettle. Sometimes he smiled and drew her close, and then he sighed
and shook his head. But she was dreaming about the
nursery and the sunflowers and the kitten, and had forgotten that the hour of the waiters' downfall was nearly
upon them.

By twos and threes the waiters came out of the wood
towards the cottage, with their heads bent against the
wind and their arms tucked in their ragged sleeves, and
gathered into a crowd. It was joined by others, until
nearly fifty were standing there, silently gazing towards the
direction whence the soldiers would come. At last there
came the distant noise of a paper-and-comb band, and the
waiters' army began to file through the trees, led by Agneo
Testetti with a clothes prop to which a carving-knife was
tied, and Scant and Gast carrying a sacking banner on
which was daubed:

ALL WE DEMAND IS JUSSTISS

"Poor souls," muttered Ticky.

"Dear Gerard, haven't you got to go on duty?" asked
Philly timidly, putting her hand on his arm.

"Not this afternoon, my dearest girl. The Colonel
knew better than to appoint me. By George! There's old
Pressure, and Madame Jeanne and Miss Beatrice, too.
Let's hope they don't want to come in here. I am in no
mood to talk to them."

Doctor Pressure's party took up a place on the edge of
the wood where the ladies could find some shelter from

the wind, and Doctor Pressure, who was wrapped in his travelling cape, took out field-glasses and surveyed the scene. He looked very grave and kept on shaking his head and muttering, "Liberty, Equality, Fraternity." Mrs. Lovecome amused herself by collecting some autumn leaves, and Beatrice looked sorrowfully at the defiant waiters and prayed that the poor misguided creatures would see the light and that Captain Gabriel might not be hurt in the bloodshed that would undoubtedly ensue if they didn't. George Licker came obsequiously forward with some hot bricks for the ladies' feet and was rewarded with twopence, and then he and his father retired to a convenient spot and George showed his father the twopence and his father patted him on the head, and they both sat down cosily upon a large old tub to await the defeat of their comrades.

The next arrivals were Bella and Badd and some of the other batmen with Father Doogood, who was rather miserable because it was such an unpleasant day and he was in such bad company. How he longed to be for once with good people, who did not drink and swear and mock at everything holy! who could play the piano properly and did not spit on the floor! However, he consoled himself by remembering that in the last fifteen years he had succeeded in getting himself admitted as a familiar member of The Bugle Blast social circle; who knew, in another fifteen he might save all their souls!

"Arthur Sobber! and all the rest of you miserable mites," shouted Augustine Thwart threateningly, "you come over 'ere at once and take up arms like men or I won't half pay you!"

There was a mutter of approval from the ranks of the waiters' army. Arthur Sobber and his adherents made hesitant excusatory gestures with their hands and shoulders but continued to stand in a mournful black group by the waiters' cemetery.

The Pleasure Gardens were now almost full of people, and the only rich colours against the dun and ashen hues of the leafless wood, the bleached beds of withered cresses, and the grey skies, were Mrs. Lovecome's crimson mantle and Beatrice's green velvet one. The army of waiters was drawn up, on the instructions of Agneo Testetti, with its back to the woods (thus making it convenient for an opposing force to cut off its rear), on the grounds that it "look-a more splendid when an army stand against a wood, like-a an old picuture in da *chiesa* in Italy, you trust-a me." The rags fluttered in the cold wind and Gast blew on his fingers that were numb with holding the banner.

The band was giving a selection of military favourites, "Drumming Dandy," "The Bugler's Farewell," "March Along, Lads," and "Lay My Bones Low;" and they had just finished rendering the last air, on a prolonged blast from Wear's comb, when a thrill of excitement swept over the crowd and every head was turned towards the wood. Wear's note died away on a quaver, and into the hush there suddenly burst the gay, heartless tune of "Waterloo Willie," the First Bloods' regimental march, played at the quickstep by the regimental band. And down the path between the trees there came, first a glow of scarlet and purple and copper winding among the leafless bushes, and then, as it emerged into the open, the full splendour of the Regiment, led by the Colonel upon his black charger and followed by Major Pillichoddie, Major Baird and the Ensigns Cussett and Dannit, with Captain Gabriel bringing up the rear, all magnificent in the purple great-coats and black astrakhan busbies of their winter dress. The violet and copper colours burned like dark jewels under the lowering sky and the remorseless gaiety of "Waterloo Willie" set every toe in the audience a-tapping. All the Men looked exceedingly cross.

The Regiment emerged almost on top of the waiters'

army and considerably upset its rear, Bone going so far as to overbalance into a ditch (fortunately dry), whence he was immediately and in passing hauled out by the enormous Private Jones, who observed out of the side of his mouth, "Nah then, me lad, mind your eye," and set him down on his feet as gently as if he were a kitten.

From his seat by the brazier, where the kettle was almost at the boil and the chestnuts were steadily blackening, Ticky watched breathlessly. Philly's warm weight leant against his shoulder and her eyes were fixed immovably upon the Regiment as it marched to the centre of the square, and Mrs. Sawyer was turning potatoes round and round without looking at what she was doing.

The Regiment halted, presented arms, and stood motionless.

The Colonel rode out in front of them, sternly and keenly surveyed the ranks, then turned his charger about, and faced the crowd and the waiters' army. He motioned to Sergeant Cannonroyal, who came forward and began to gabble from a paper which he held in front of him as if he personally disliked it.

CHAPTER XXX

"DRILL Ground Number Eight, hitherto known as the Pleasure Gardens, is about to be taken over by the First Bloods Regiment and added to the grounds of the Club. Notice is hereby given to any persons who may have taken squatter's presumption thereon that all goods, living or inanimate, must be finally removed within the next hour."

The Sergeant drew a deep breath, saluted, rolled up the paper, and stepped back.

For a moment there was silence. Desperation seemed to hover in the air. The waiters moved and muttered among themselves and one or two stepped half-heartedly forward from the ranks. A faint wailing noise began in the cemetery, where the waiters' wives had taken cover. Ticky stood up, clutching his handkerchief between his hands, and staring.

The Colonel motioned to Sergeant Cannonroyal, who, after a hesitation so slight that only the men nearest to him saw it and held their breath, again stepped forward.

"The Pleasure Gardens," he roared sullenly, "will now be hannexed."

The Colonel lifted his hand, and opened his mouth to proclaim the annexation.

At that instant a horse dashed out of the woods at a gallop and every eye was turned to see whom the rider might be. It was Major Milde. Spurring the charger forward, he reached the Colonel in a few seconds, drew rein, and saluted.

"Sir, pray forgive this unpardonable intrusion at so solemn a time," he began, in a ringing voice full of authority and power, completely unlike his usual diffident tones, "I have come to beg a favour."

"A favour, Major Milde!" The Colonel drew himself up with a haughty frown; his voice was lower than Major Milde's, but so clear that every word could be heard by the breathlessly watching and listening crowd. "At this hour?"

"Yes, sir," retorted Major Milde.

"Not for more leave, I trust, Major Milde?" The Colonel's voice was terrible to hear.

"No, indeed, sir." Major Milde wheeled his charger about so that he partly faced the waiters and the crowd, "not for more leave. I shall never again ask for leave, save on those occasions when it is due to me. No, Colonel Delawarre; I have come to beg you to hold your hand."

"To hold my hand, sirrah? To hold my hand?"

"Yes, sir. To leave the Pleasure Gardens to these humble and innocent men, as their fathers had it before them."

A subdued cheer came from some of the waiters at this, but most of them were too furious at being called humble and innocent to utter a sound.

"*Indeed*, Major Milde? And by what right do you ask such a thing?"

"By right of my services to the Regiment, sir. I ask," and here Major Milde flung up his arm and raised his voice, "in the name of The Wolf!"

A murmur of amazement went up from the crowd, increasing and growing so loud that for a moment the Colonel could not make his voice heard above it. Everyone was leaning forward to try to get a closer view of Major Milde, the waiters had broken their ranks, and while the Regiment still stood immovably at attention the faces of the men expressed the liveliest interest and amazement.

"The—The Wolf?" stammered Colonel Delawarre.

"Ay, The Wolf. Sir, my task is done. For five years, ever since my seven daughters came to the estate of womanhood, I have set myself to procure for them portions which should, added to their undoubted charms, settle each comfortably in life with the man of her choice. All of you who are fathers, all of you whose means are modest"
—he flung out his arms—"will, I know, understand."

Sympathetic and approving murmurs were heard on all sides, but not too loud, for fear of missing a word.

"By apprehending various savage criminals both here and in Hindostan I have secured the rewards offered for their capture. Each of my daughters now has a portion, and therefore my task is completed. I may fling off the mask, I need ask for no more leave in order to track down and capture my prey, and I can reveal to you all that I, and no other, am The Wolf!''

At this the discipline of the soldiers was swept away and led by Sergeant Cannonroyal they flung their busbies in the air, shouting again and again:

"The Wolf, God bless 'im. Three cheers for The Wolf!'' and a like demonstration, but even more heartfelt, came from the waiters.

The Colonel attempted once or twice to speak but could not make himself heard above the cheering. When he did succeed in doing so, he spoke with some embarrassment.

"A surprise indeed, Major Milde, but a most welcome one. You have indeed added lustre to the annals of the Regiment and in its name I most heartily congratulate you.''

Major Milde saluted.

"And my request, sir? You will take into consideration my achievements—such as they are—and reward them by permitting the waiters to retain their rights in these Pleasure Gardens?''

The waiters' army, with hopelessly disorganized ranks, pressed breathlessly forward to hear the answer.

It was at this precise moment that habit was too strong for Mrs. Sawyer, whom we left in the cottage with Ticky and Philly. In spite of her intense interest in the drama that was going on, she observed out of the corner of her eye that the kettle was about to boil over.

Not being in a position to reach it herself, for she was in a far corner near the door, she leant over and pulled at Ticky's sleeve.

"Lieutenant Toloreaux! The kettle!'' she whispered urgently. Ticky was still, in his excitement, kneading between his palms the object which he assumed to be his handkerchief, and did not hear her.

The Colonel's voice rang hard and clear in answer.

"I regret, Major Milde, that in spite of my admiration for your exploits and the glory they have added to the Regiment, I must decline to grant your request."

A moan went up from the waiters.

"Lieutenant Toloreaux! Take the kettle off!" whispered Mrs. Sawyer, more urgently.

"Is this your last word, sir?" demanded Major Milde.

"It is, Major Milde."

"Then," Major Milde turned to the waiters, "I fear I can do no more, my good friends. I have done all I could——"

"Thass all right, sir."

"The Wolf, God bless 'im!"

"You done your best, sir. No malice borne——"

"——And Might must prove once more to be Right," concluded Major Milde sorrowfully.

Dismayed at what he heard, half-conscious of Mrs. Sawyer's sharp instructions, Ticky glanced down at the object he was holding. It was not his handkerchief, it was the kettle-holder. He heard the Colonel's loud voice begin: "I hereby, in the name of our Beloved and Reverend Sovereign Victoria, Queen of Great Britain and Ireland——" in the opening words of the traditional Act of Annexation, and then, as he stupidly stared down at the kettle-holder, he found other words echoing in his head:

"Freedom, Peace and Plenty . . . to have and to hold . . . for as long as the Regiment shall endure. . . ."

But the words were not sounding in his head, he was reading them; they were before his eyes; he was staring down at the kettle-holder, and they were written in black letters on its parchment back. For a moment longer he stupidly stared at them.

Then he sprang up and tore out of the cottage, and raced across the Pleasure Gardens like a madman, shouting and waving the kettle-holder over his head. Right between the ranks of the cowering waiters he ran, past the crowd, up to the Regiment as it stood there sullenly awaiting the end of the Annexation Act, under the astonished faces of his brother officers, to the Colonel himself.

He thrust the kettle-holder under his nose.

"Read that!" he gasped. "*Read* it!"

It was the missing Charter.

CHAPTER XXXI

THE Colonel stared at the blackened object, then slowly put out his hand and took it from Ticky's trembling one. In the midst of the sudden hush that had fallen upon the crowd, he began to read.

But before he had read a word, his face had grown white and set itself into a frozen calm. He knew what he held in his hand. He knew that Providence, at the eleventh moment of the eleventh hour, had for its own inscrutable reasons seen fit to snatch the Pleasure Gardens from his hand. He knew that he was defeated, and even while he read the hatefully familiar sentences his mind was racing, trying to find a way in which he could gracefully get out of the jam.

It did not take him more than three minutes to peruse the document, but in that time, in some mysterious way, the waiters knew. A sort of convulsion passed over them. Scant fell on the ground in a faint and had to be madly fanned by Skinner; Agneo Testetti was sharply slapped down b Augustine Thwart as he began to fling his top-hat into the air, and a silent but desperate struggle started among the comb-and-paper band, some of whose members wanted to burst forthwith into "Now Thank We All Our God." The Men were again standing at attention but they were all smiling broadly, and hysterical peals of laughter and ejaculations of "There, Johnny, now you won't 'ave to play in the streets!" and "Thank 'eavens!" came faintly on the wind from the direction of the cemetery. Doctor Pressure had quickly put on a look of grave relief, tempered with regret at the Colonel's disappointment, and Major Milde and Major Pillichoddie were exchanging thankful glances. And Ticky's warm heart was quite overflowing with joy. He stood in the bitter wind without his busby, for it had fallen off in his headlong dash across the Pleasure Gardens, agitatedly grasping the reins of the Colonel's charger, while he gazed anxiously up into the Colonel's pale, expressionless face.

At last the Colonel lifted his head and spoke, and although his words were pleasant the tone was bitter as quinine; Sergeant Cannonroyal said afterwards it brought back all Miss Nightingale's draughts and pills just to listen to it.

"Ladies and gentlemen, officers and men of the First Bloods, and waiters in attendance upon the Club premises," began the Colonel, "I have some good news for you. It gives me much pleasure to be the bearer of it. Here"—and he held up the kettle-holder—"is your missing Charter!"

But at this a disgraceful scene occurred. The men broke ranks and rushed across to the waiters, dropping their rifles as they ran, and roaring, "What-cher, cocks! Congraturuddylations!" Many waiters were felled to the earth by the force of the soldiers' back-slappings, and others leant against trees sobbing into their tattered sleeves. Some took hands and danced madly round and round shrieking, "We won't be home till morning," while the five who had been going to brain the Colonel with the flinty jam-jars flung them aside and started leap-frogging to and fro over each other's backs. Agneo Testetti kissed Arthur Sobber, who had snatched off his mourning robe and was waving it round his head like a banner and cheering madly. Scant had recovered from his swoon and was shouting deliriously, "Wasn't my old mother right?" while Dearth, the other waiter who had never despaired in the darkest hour, was rushing from one frenzied group to another demanding, "Didn't I say it would all come right? My Pa was a gipsy, and I knew."

Even Badd and Emmy, though desirous of giving no offence to the Colonel, were infected by the general rejoicing and were clapping their hands as if at a performance of Blondin's, and tears of happiness were running down Father Doogood's face. "*So* nice for the poor creatures," observed Mrs. Lovecome, smilingly surveying the scene. "Quite like one of dear Miss Braddon's stories —although, personally, I prefer Ouida—you really must read Ouida after you are married, Beatrice."

Only Captain Gabriel looked grave; his kind heart could not help rejoicing at the sight of so much happiness, but he deplored the loss to the Regiment of the new drill ground and also the defeat of his Colonel's hopes. Beatrice, observing his sober looks, made her little face sober, too.

Barry, copying the Colonel, looked white and sour. ("Sh'd 'ave thought it were too cold to-day to turn the cream, wouldn't you, Piddler?" guffawed Private Mack with a glance at Barry, as he went leisurely back towards what was left of the ranks.) The Colonel, sitting white and still upon his charger, had been roaring out commands for the past five minutes.

When at last order was restored, and waiters and soldiers were separated into their own ranks again, the Colonel, whose nose seemed made of wax, held up his hand for silence. It fell immediately; indeed, Mrs. Sawyer, who was feverishly setting out her potatoes and

chestnuts with some rattling of pans in anticipation of a
roaring trade later, received indignant glances.

"I will make allowances for some natural excitement,"
announced the Colonel freezingly, "and none of you,
despite the astounding and unprecedented scenes that I
have just witnessed, will be arrested or shot." He paused,
but instead of the grateful murmur which he had expected
he got nothing but a loud hand-clap from the two Lickers,
which he immediately quelled with one look. He went
on in tones which he tried to make jovial. "As the Charter
has been found, the Pleasure Gardens will not, of course,
be annexed." He paused again. Was there, or was there
not, a murmur of "*I should ruddy well fink not indeed*"
from the waiters' ranks? "They now belong, in perpetuity,
to the—er—to the Club servants, who, so I understand,
have some squatter's presumption thereon. I shall now
bestow the restored Charter on the—er—the appointed
representative of the Club servants, if he will step forward."

Almost before the words were out of his mouth,
Augustine Thwart was under the charger's nose and
silently holding up a large dirty hand.

"Ah—yes—indeed. Er—here it is, then," observed
the Colonel, drawing back a little.

"Thenks," said Augustine Thwart, who was more than
a bit above himself. "Sir," he added.

"I would suggest that in future the Charter be kept in
some safe place," observed the Colonel, eyeing it as it
rested in Augustine Thwart's hand. "The Regimental
Archives Room is practically impregnable."

"Yus, we knows, sir," spoke up Thwart, backing rather
quickly towards the waiters' ranks. "Thanking you
and the other gents all the same, sir, we'll keep it ourselves."

"Indeed? And pray, where will you keep it?"
demanded the Colonel playfully, with a whiter nose than
ever.

"That's tellings, sir," retorted Augustine Thwart promptly, in a perfect frenzy of impertinence and triumph, and a murmur of approval came from the waiters' ranks, while Gast was suddenly sick from excitement and had to be hustled away.

"And just to demonstrate how relieved I am that the matter has been adjusted in the way it has," continued the Colonel, "I am prepared to disburse out of the Regimental Funds the sum of one thousand pounds for the purposes of paving over the Pleasure Gardens, providing a ragged school for the juveniles (if any such there be), uprooting the unhealthy ancient trees, draining the marsh, and building a combined Refreshment Room and Penny Reading Hall, where the tea and buns will be provided by the man Licker and his son, and the Penny Readings by Doctor Harrovius Pressure, Headmaster of the First Bloods' Military Preparatory School." (Here Doctor Pressure started, and gazed indignantly at the Colonel, while upon his lips the words "What of my work upon *Molassus the Younger*?" shaped themselves.)

But he need have had no cause for alarm. After some dismayed mutterings among themselves that contrasted curiously with the approving faces and gratified murmurs of the gentry, the waiters pushed forth forward Arthur Sobber (Augustine Thwart having been suddenly overcome by reaction and fright and retreated with the Charter to the back of the crowd). Sobber, though faint with terror, piped up:

"Thanking you and the other gents all the same, sir, but we'd rather 'ave it as it is."

"What?" exclaimed the Colonel as if unable to believe what he heard.

"Thass right, sir," cried a dozen thin voices.

"The swamp—the unhealthy coppice where pestilence lingers—the rugged uneven ground—the absence of all wholesome refreshment for the body and—more precious still—for the mind?" exclaimed the Colonel. "You prefer the place *as it is*?"

"Thass right, sir," cried the voices again.

There was a prolonged pause.

"It is no more," suddenly said the Colonel, very finally and bitterly, "than I expected. Well, be it so. Come, gentlemen, our business here is done." He turned his horse and spurred it forward. "Eyes right! Forward—march!"

The brilliant procession, led by the officers on their black chargers, moved rapidly away towards the little wood and vanished among its trees. Evening was now at hand, and as soon as the last notes of "Waterloo Willie" had died away, the red glow from Mrs. Sawyer's brazier shone forth from her cottage. How light were the hearts of those who crowded round to buy the floury hot potatoes and the mellow chestnuts rolled in salt! How merrily the saloop went down, and the scalding tea! Ticky sat by the brazier with its red glow on his fair curly hair and his arm around Philly's waist, and told them over and over again how he had looked down, at the very instant the Colonel began to proclaim the Act of Annexation, and seen the Charter clasped in his hands. It did indeed seem a miracle.

"Specially favoured, thass what we are," said Skinner solemnly to Wear, as the waiters set out for the North Tower an hour later to prepare themselves for their evening's duties. "Chosen, thass what. 'Ow long is it since there was a miracle in London? Not since the Thames froze over."

"Makes yer think, don't it, though?"

"Not 'alf. By the way, where's the Charter?"

"Oh, Gawd, 'aven't you got it? I thought you 'ad."

"You mean *I* thought *you* 'ad. You 'ad, too. Come on, where is it? Gast, 'ave you got it?"

"S'elp me, I 'aven't. Testetti, 'ave you got the blinkin' Charter?"

"Neva- have-a seen since-a Thwart have it."

"*Oh, Gawd, it's lost!*"

"Shut your row, all of you," came the severe and reassuring voice of Augustine Thwart out of the darkness. "I got it."

"Oh, thang Gawd! Are yer sure, mate?"

"Of course I'm sure."

"Where is it? Somewhere safe?"

"I 'ope so. Down me trousers."

CHAPTER XXXII

AFTER the events described in the previous chapter, everybody was thankful to settle down for three weeks or so and discuss what had happened, while gathering up their strength to attend the nuptials of Doctor Pressure and his daughter. There was plenty to talk about, and a minor excitement was the announcement that Lieutenant Toloreaux had purchased his release from the Regiment and would be married to Philly Sawyer on the same day that witnessed the socially more lofty plightings of Doctor Pressure and Captain Gabriel Venner.

There was great rejoicing and pleasure over this in the Waiters' Quarters, where Ticky had always been popular and since his discovery of the missing Charter was regarded as a kind of idol. One of the waiters named Fig Starkadder, a gloomy man reputed to come from Sussex, had a talent for drawing and was already at work upon a vast new fresco depicting the discovery of the Charter. The novelty about this was that the actual Charter itself, enclosed in a small hole covered by a movable pane of glass, was resting in the painted hand of the Ticky depicted

upon the wall. A waiter was always on sentry-go beneath **the fresco, guarding** the precious object, but as a ladder **stood beside him,** which anybody could run up to take a peep at the Charter and refresh themselves whenever they were feeling low, and as on these occasions they always took it out "just to 'ave a feel of it, like," it is doubtful whether the Charter was any safer in its new home than it had been in its old one.

Doctor Pressure, animated by a scholar's interest in the viscissitudes of an historical document, had so far roused himself from his absorption in *Molassus the Younger* to institute some inquiries about the Charter's wanderings. Unable, naturally, to descend himself into such a low place as Mrs. Sawyer's cottage, he had dispatched the unhappy Bodder thither, instructing him to question Mrs. Sawyer minutely as to how she first acquired the kettle-holder, and when.

The reader may recall that the kettle-holder had originally been a small banner, embroidered with the words "Cursed be the Colonel," and presented to Mrs. Sawyer by some of the waiters' wives on the first anniversary of her husband's death. Mrs. Sawyer explained to the shrinking Bodder that she used at first to bring it out once a week and hang it on the wall, but gradually she got out of the habit ("there being always such a deal to do, dear") and somehow, in the haste of preparing shrimps and boiling water for tea, the banner passed into use as a kettle-holder. Bodder, making notes in a penny book, stiffly inquired if she could provide him with the names and addresses of the waiters' wives who had presented her with the banner, and after some meditation she did recall one or two names, including those of Mrs. Dearth and Mrs. Scant.

As an old man in after years, Bodder would never speak in detail about his visit to the homes of the waiters' wives. He would only shudder and hastily drink down whatever happened to be nearest and most palatable, and then relate how, after an absence of four days, he had staggered into Doctor Pressure's study, starving and with nothing on but a sack, and fainted at his master's feet. But with him he brought enough verbal evidence to prove that the Charter must have been knocking about the Scant home for many years; ever since, in fact, the days of that old Mrs. Scant, who Scant had always sworn would soon have found the Charter had she still been alive. No doubt the waiter's verdict of "*So old Ma Scant 'ad it all the time! Those oo 'ide* can *find!*" was a crude one, but it was as near the truth, Doctor Pressure decided, as he would ever get; and, having rewarded Bodder with two shillings for his pains, he embodied the facts in his *Short History of the Club Servants' Charter*, and considered the matter closed.

The Colonel believed Ticky to be responsible for the whole affair, and was unshakably convinced that he had been carrying the Charter round in his pocket for weeks. This suspicion did much to lessen his opposition, though not his anger, when Ticky wrote to him requesting permission to buy himself out of the Regiment. He gave the required consent in an icily worded note; an offer from Ticky to add fifty pounds to the necessary sum "if I may have my uniform and wear it sometimes on Sundays as my betrothed, Miss Sawyer, *delights* to see me in it" he very properly ignored. Nor would he give permission for Ticky and Philly to be married in the Chapel with Doctor Pressure and Captain Gabriel, but directed Major Pillichoddie to inform Ticky that he must be married from a small booth set up in the Pleasure Gardens, as the waiters were always married—"since Lieutenant Toloreaux so affects the society of waiters."

Much Ticky cared. He had engaged the sympathetic interest of Mrs. Lovecome in himself and his sweetheart, and Mrs. Lovecome had presented Philly with a cheque for fifty guineas as a wedding present, and also the loveliest wedding-dress, which only needed a little enlarging; snow-white velvet and fourteen yards round the crinoline, and a wreath of orange blossom made from pearls!

The reason for this was:

"But, my darling Beatrice, M. Worth has *designed* and *made* this dress especially for you, after studying your likeness. He will be very offended indeed if you refuse to wear it."

"I grieve very much to seem ungrateful to you, Mamma, but indeed, *indeed*, I cannot disappoint Miss Tucker. She has always made all my gowns."

"I know, dearest."

"—And she would never recover from the shock, I fear, if I wore a wedding-dress made by a stranger."

"Beatrice! M. Worth is hardly a stranger!"

"He is to me, dear Mamma. And beautiful though this gown is, I would sooner wear the one which Miss Tucker has prepared."

"Prepared! As if it were a soup!"

"I shall be so happy, what does it matter what gown I wear?"

"My darling! Of course, it is your wedding, and you shall wear what you please. (Oh, what a worldly woman I am!) But white lawn! And all those tucks! And *still* not fitting anywhere! You will look like a dear little candle!"

"Darling Mamma, you will see my eyes shining like the candle's light when it is put in the window to welcome someone home, and you will not mind any more."

At which Mrs. Lovecome kissed her and rushed away into the dressing-room to cry, while Sour, who had never stopped crying since the engagement was announced, began to pack up the wedding-dress for that piece, Philly Sawyer.

At last the wedding-day came. The morning was a

peculiarly beautiful one, for on the previous night there had been a heavy white frost and every tree was cased in glistening rime, while the ground was covered with silver. There was mist in the air, and the sun shone through it in a fainting hue of gold that was impossible to detect in one place, yet pervaded every motionless shrub and all the strangely bright air. The big trees were armoured in white, with blue shadows flowing out at their roots, and their highest branches, where blackbirds sat motionless, were glistening with gold. The lawns sparkled out tiny colours of red, green and blue, and the Gothic arches of the barracks and the mighty twin towers of the Club looked like ornaments for a wedding-cake.

The Hon. Theodule de Wincie, the Colonel's nephew and heir, had arrived on the previous night for the festivities, and was now strolling about in the frost, with his green velvet cloak open wide and his notebook in hand, while he made some sketches with pastel chalks as notes for future paintings. Half the Men were hanging about the barracks trying to get a glimpse of him, for rumours had got around, and it was said that the Colonel was trying to persuade him to enter the Regiment and be trained to take command of it when the Colonel should reach the age of retirement. As Mr. de Wincie lived in a castle in the country with a very old mother and three very old aunts of great sensibility (the de Wincie family motto was "*All—all, all, all, all Heart*") and artistic taste, and as they were reliably reported to be unable to eat the bread and butter for tea unless it was cut so thin that it floated away on the breeze as the butler carried it along the picture gallery, the curiosity of the Men is understandable.

Mr. de Wincie continued to peer under bushes and scribble and to stare at the sky and scrawl, and the Men (unmoved by the spectacle of a completely happy human being) continued to gawp at him and to find their juiciest fears, from his clean-shaven cheeks to his baggy velveteen trousers, no worse than the truth.

All over the Club, the Barracks, the Pleasure Gardens and the Waiters' Quarters, there was an increasing bustle of pleasurable preparations as the morning wore on. The waiters were feverishly polishing their top-hats, and some of them were putting the finishing touches to the rickety canvas booth, roughly daubed to look like brick, in which many generations of waiters had been married and in which Ticky and Philly were this day to be united by the Rev. H. Plainsong (the others, of course, were to be married by a bishop).

"Mum, do I look all right?"

"As pretty as a fresh shrimp, my girl."

"Oh, Mum, you are mean!"

"Well, hold your tongue for five minutes; I've got you all trimmed up and ready and now I want to fix this here feather for meself."

Philly went to the door and pulled aside the sacking that had been affixed there to conceal her from public view while she dressed, and looked out. The icy air, silver and gold with frost and sunlight, touched her pink cheeks and plump bare shoulders and Mrs. Sawyer, without looking up from her task, threw her a shawl with a mutter, "That's right; now get the pewmonia." Just as she put it on, Father Doogood passed by, escorting Bella, and stopped to speak to her.

"Sure, it's grieved I am that I cannot be afther celebrating your wedding, Miss Sawyer, us being of different faiths, but I can give ye my blessing and that I will do with all my heart."

"Oh, thank you, Father Doogood," and Philly knelt down in the cottage door and shut her eyes and clasped her hands. Just as her knees touched the ground she felt a mat slide between them and the stone, and when she opened her eyes after the blessing, they met the eyes of Bella.

"Didn't want you to soil that lovely creation on the dirty floor, dearie," said Bella in a hoarse whisper. "And let's hope you'll make a better success of the holy estate than what I did, that's all I got to say, and for a bit longer, too. Now come on, Father, or we shan't get good seats," and she bustled Father Doogood off before Philly could say "thank you." Fancy, thought Philly. That was kind of her. I suppose everybody's kind sometimes.

Major Pillichoddie had just finished saying his prayers (he had quite got into the habit recently) after a late breakfast and was now standing still while his batman finished his toilet. His meditations were of the gloomiest, for he was still out of favour with Her Majesty, and the Colonel's manner to him, though slightly less forbidding than it had been, was still far from polite, let alone friendly. Deuce take it, and I can't even frequent the pot-house since there was all that to-do, thought the Major, raising his chin while his man adjusted his collar. And everybody gettin' married and givin' up their commissions; don't know what the Regiment's comin' to at all. "Dammet, man, are you trying to stifle me?"

"Sorry, sir."

Cussett and Dannit, as was their custom on such occasions, were laying a number of indelicate wagers on the results of the day's events, which need not be recorded here.

The ceremonies were timed to begin at half-past twelve; and at half-past eleven the Colonel, who had been chatting in his apartments with Cardinal Baldaccio, an old Italian friend and prelate who was visiting him, suddenly experienced one of his changes of heart. Curse it, I am a man of feeling, he thought, while his batman sprayed him with a perfume named *Blood and Iron*, which had been especially created in Paris for a lady friend of Bismarck's. Can I witness the ceremony that will be solemnized to-day, and remain unmoved? Damn it, no.

And who knows? Should Venner have eight healthy boys or so the Regiment will get 'em all. Blast it, the affair shall go forward with my blessing. And he was smiling as he came gracefully down the great staircase half an hour later, causing Private Snoot, who was on sentry-go at the bottom of it, to think, "Oh, Gawd, 'ere comes the laughing hyena, so look out for yourselves."

The Colonel strode across the frosty grounds to the chapel, where almost a hundred guests were already assembled. The sacred edifice was decorated with wreaths of orange blossom and mistletoe: of these floral messages only Lady Venner and Cardinal Baldaccio were sufficiently worldly to know the meaning, and the two, after one glance, were careful not to catch each other's eyes. The choice was Mrs. Lovecome's, and Doctor Pressure, who was to pay it, had not yet been confronted with the bill.

A large marquee had been set up at the entrance to the Chapel, as the latter was not big enough to contain both the young gentlemen from the Military Preparatory School and the young ladies from Mrs. Lovecome's Academy. The two schools were now seated in the marquee, one on either side of it, with a master and mistress from each establishment to keep them in order. A brisk business in bunches of flowers, peppermint hearts, valentines and notes of assignation was being done under the noses of these two unfortunates, who were kept ceaselessly busy darting backwards and forwards slapping at people and giving them lines and otherwise trying to avert the course of Nature.

Major Pillichoddie, dejectedly settling himself for a preliminary prayer into his busby, was surprised to be hailed by the Colonel, who was passing on his way to his own place near the altar.

"Ha, Hugo! Don't want to hide yourself away down there, man; come up near the front with me, eh?"

"By all means, Eustace," replied Major Pillichoddie,

with some embarrassment, but he got up and pushed his way past satin and broadcloth knees and interested faces, and followed the Colonel as he strode down the aisle to a sort of bower all done up with red muslin and the Union Jack and palms in pots. Good Gad, it looks like a box at Astley's, have we got to sit in that? What monkeys we shall look, thought the Major, but as the Colonel apparently saw nothing amiss—indeed, he gave the palms a caressing glance—he followed him into the contraption. In one corner of it sat a young man exquisitely attired in morning dress and a pale lilac velvet cape, who was leaning back and inhaling, with his eyes shut, the fumes of a pastille burning in a little bowl.

"My nephew, Theodule de Wincie," said the Colonel, indicating the young man. "Major Pillichoddie."

"Charmed and delighted," murmured Mr. de Wincie, opening his eyes and putting down the little bowl and looking earnestly at the Major. "Such a happy, *happy* occasion, is it not?"

"Most gratifying, indeed," whispered the Major, relieved to find that Mr. de Wincie, unlike his uncle, paid the sacred edifice the compliment of lowering his voice while he was sitting in it.

"Will you refresh yourself?" asked Mr. de Wincie, holding out the little bowl to the Major, who drew back muttering, "Good G——, no, I thank you, sir."

"Ha, ha! Hugo is an old war-dog, you mustn't expect him to appreciate such refinements," exclaimed the Colonel, sitting down and stretching out his legs while he ran a critical eye over the altar and another little red muslin booth immediately opposite the one in which they sat. This one had a gilt crown over the top and a lot of red roses in it.

"Yes, Her Majesty proposes to honour us with her presence," the Colonel added, as the Major followed his glance towards the gilt crown.

"An honour, indeed," said Major Pillichoddie gruffly. "Most gratifyin'."

"Barbarian blood," whispered Mr. de Wincie, leaning back and shutting his eyes. "Visigoths and Huns."

"My nephew is in favour of restoring the succession to the original English line—that is, to the Welsh, as they now are," confided the Colonel.

Major Pillichoddie was silent. His pleasure at being restored to the Colonel's good graces was almost lost in his dismay at the prospect of Mr. de Wincie entering the Regiment and one day, perhaps, taking the Colonel's place. After some reflection the Major said another prayer into his busby.

On the wooden benches outside the booth in the Pleasure Gardens a great crowd of waiters was assembled, together with as many of the Men as could get away from the barracks, all the waiters' wives in their best shawls and bonnets (many of them not worn since Queen Adelaide's funeral) and the waiters' children in prams made from sugar-boxes. The Rev. H. Plainsong was already standing in the booth, almost hidden by the splendid branches of holly, thick with shiny red berries, that decorated it. Over the altar (also made from a sugar-box) was a bough of the shower-like winter jasmine, with its yellow flowers and delicious scent, both holly and jasmine having been provided by that waiter's sister who had a garden at Barnet. A narrow carpet of sacking, dyed red by the waiters' wives and bordered by flowerpots filled with cockle-shells, ran down between the benches for the bridal procession to walk on. These arrangements had that curiously satisfying effect produced by the simplest objects when cleanliness and design have been rigidly imposed upon them. It had not been possible to impose these qualities upon the two little bridesmaids, whose dresses were fashioned from a tablecloth stolen from the Mess; nevertheless, their appearance was generally agreed to be pleasing.

On the edge of the Pleasure Gardens stood Bone, with a white flag in his hand, and in receding procession so far as the eye could discern them stood other waiters also carrying flags. By this simple method of communication the Rev. H. Plainsong would know the precise second at which the Bishop would begin the ceremony in the Chapel (the Bishop, of course, did not care when the Rev. H. Plainsong began) and could start marrying Ticky and Philly. The waiters and all Ticky's supporters and friends were most anxious that the two ceremonies should take place simultaneously. The only circumstance that marred the day's pleasure was the fact that it was not possible to attend both ceremonies at once, and it was generally agreed that no one but the Colonel could have thought up such a simple but fiendishly effective method of putting a fly into the collective ointment.

Mrs. Lovecome's carriage was proceeding at a walking pace across the Club grounds. She herself, in an amber velvet wedding-dress and cap of old yellow Spanish lace, was smelling at her bouquet of tea-roses and savouring the triumph and happiness of her wedding-day, when Sir Alastair Venner, who was to give her away, leant towards her from his seat opposite and observed:

"Jeanne, my dear, a young fellow seems to be trying to catch your eye. Shall I draw the curtains?"

Without lifting her head, she looked up over the roses. Barry had come up on Bayard and was now riding by the carriage, busby in hand, looking down at her in silence. For once Mrs. Lovecome was at a loss, and, after some thought, all she could do was to wave the roses feebly at him and give a weak smile.

"I wish you all happiness," said Barry softly, while the horse paced steadily beside the carriage. "In a few weeks, at my own request, I leave for Afghanistan. It is a country as yet hardly touched by the march of progress, and I am going into its savage heart."

Mrs. Lovecome continued to stare at him over the roses, trying to think of a suitable comment.

"My life is in ruins," he went on hoarsely. "Have you *nothing* to say to me?"

Here Sir Alastair, explosively uttering "t-t-t-t——" got up to shut the window, but Mrs. Lovecome stopped him.

"I am very sorry," she said faintly, "but it wasn't my fault."

Barry laughed bitterly, then bent over his horse's neck and before she could guess his intention, wrenched a rose from the heart of her bouquet.

"Good-bye for ever," he said, and thrusting the flower into the breast of his uniform, he set the spurs into his horse and galloped away.

". . . Never saw such an ill-bred thing in all my life!" fumed Sir Alastair, fanning her with his hat. "Enough to kill a delicate woman on her wedding morning. Young cub! I hope the Afghans may knife him. Your charming bouquet, too, my dear! It is all disarranged."

"He is a very foolish boy, but I have hopes he is not so deeply affected as he appears to be," she returned composedly, relieved that Sir Alastair apparently attached no blame to herself. "A hopeless passion does a young man no harm, my dear friend, and I trust to the more bracing air of Afghanistan to cure him."

Sir Alastair was understood to mutter that all the same he should deuced well see that Eustace heard of the matter, and Mrs. Lovecome occupied herself with rearranging her bouquet as best she could until the Chapel was reached.

It was now nearly half-past twelve. The Bishop was refreshing himself by a final peep at the Bible in a little room at the back of the organ. Miss Tucker was kneeling in the porch arranging the white muslin train (one layer thick, with six daisies made by Miss Tucker's three work-girls scattered hither and thither upon it) of Beatrice's wedding-dress. Gabriel stood by the altar, grave and noble, with his heart in his kind eyes, waiting for his bride, with Major Milde fussing around him, acting as a best man but looking much more like a tug. In another little room at the back of the organ, Bodder, still weak from his wanderings among the waiters' wives, was cowering before the wrath of the other bridegroom, Doctor Pressure, whose braces had burst. The only thing to tie them up with was a sort of purple rope, apparently part of some sacred vestment, that hung on the wall and was undoubtedly one of the props. of Cardinal Baldaccio. Would it be sacrilege so to use it? While Doctor Pressure struggled with his conscience and Bodder cowered, the inexorable moments ticked on, and suddenly, to his extreme horror, Doctor Pressure heard the organ burst into the National Anthem. The Queen was arriving.

Snatching up the purple rope he tied it round himself, muttered, "I owe no respect to Popish mummeries," shook his fist at Bodder, and stepped gravely out round the organ.

He was in time to see the Queen favour Major Pillichoddie with a gracious inclination of the head and the Hon. Theodule de Wincie with a very sharp glance. Then Her Majesty knelt in prayer. In a moment the two brides were floating down the aisle towards their grooms, Beatrice upon the arm of Major Baird, who was to give her away. Each in her way was the personification of virgin and riper loveliness, and a murmur of admiration passed over the congregation.

Then the Bishop raised his white hands and great lawn sleeves, a hush fell, the waiter on duty outside the chapel dropped his flag, and the Rev. H. Plainsong inclined his head over Ticky and Philly, who were kneeling before him. The winter sunlight glinted upon Ticky's fair curls and gilded the white velvet of Philly's wedding-dress.

Then, simultaneously to the second, the two ceremonies began.

Afterwards, there was a feast of champagne and chicken in the marquee, and of hot oysters and porter in Mrs. Sawyer's cottage, and everybody enjoyed themselves and the occasion immensely.

Nobody could ever afterwards explain how it happened, but at some stage in the festivities the two banquets overflowed into one another's territories and mingled; and Mr. de Wincie might have been observed complimenting Philly, while Mrs. Sawyer was praised for her oysters by Major Baird, and so on and so forth. The only untoward incident was an attempt by Cardinal Baldaccio to bless Agneo Testetti which the latter, as a son of the New Italy, indignantly resisted. And this, it was agreed, only added to the general enjoyment. The comb-and-paper band that had played Ticky and Philly into the booth took turn about with the regimental band to render such favourites as "Drumming Dandy" and "The Bugler's Farewell," and later on there was dancing in the marquee.

Later, the mist came up so thick that they could scarcely see one another's laughing faces; and later still, at sunset, the two processions moved onwards, through the golden haze, towards the distant splendour of the Diamond Jubilee.

THE END